"Just what are we talking about here, Captain?" Jessie inquired. "It sounds like the sort of trouble that brought me here."

"Oh, there's more pirating every season, Miss Starbuck," Thorpe replied, "but it's been relatively petty stuff, hit-or-miss small bands. Creoles, renegade Indians, whites, all colors. No threat to a vessel the size and speed of the *Dauphine* on the water. They've been limited to pirogues and flat-bottom skiffs that can vanish into the bayous in minutes. Now, if somehow they've gotten financing for steam launches, it could be a different story. But there've been no reports of such attacks."

"There's always a first time," Ki said.

◆ WESLEY ELLIS ◆

LONE STAR

AND THE
RIVERBOAT GAMBLERS

J ®

A JOVE BOOK

LONE STAR AND THE RIVERBOAT GAMBLERS

A Jove book / published by arrangement with
the author

PRINTING HISTORY
Jove edition / November 1984

ISBN: 0-515-07916-2

Jove books are published by The Berkley Publishing Group,
200 Madison Avenue, New York, N.Y. 10016. The words
"A JOVE BOOK" and the "J" with sunburst are trademarks
belonging to Jove Publications, Inc.

PRINTED IN THE UNITED STATES OF AMERICA

Chapter 1

There was nothing particularly notable about the affray that began shortly after nine o'clock on that steaming evening in August, 1880, aboard the paddlewheel steam packet *Dauphine*, save that it more or less served to mark the craft's entry into the northernmost section of that legendary region called Acadiana.

Cajun country.

Here the sluggish Mississippi was the wide brown dividing line between the two cultures that had come to dominate Louisiana. To the East the influence was Spanish-Anglo; to the West, French, brought all the way from frigid Canada by the displaced Acadians, the Cajuns.

Flat terrain here, rising a few feet above the marshes, the bayous. Salt-dome islands pushing upward thousands of feet from the roiling bowels of the earth below, giving a false impression of real land under the rich alluvial accumulation deposited by the river.

There was a heady, funereal heaviness to the air, a mingling of damp marsh odors with the fragrances of myriad flora: wisteria, roses, lilies, camellias, azaleas, magnolias, oleanders, all sweetening the stink of raw petroleum seeping from the bogs. If the dark waters moved at all on the bayous, it was with sullen sluggishness. Manmade landmarks, such as had survived the War of Rebellion which had ended fifteen years before, were most noticeably the great plantation homes erected by antebellum gentry. Few of the gentry themselves had survived.

The occasional mansion, with its dependencies, bulked above the riverbanks on either side. Some were little more than moldering ruins, leaking as they sheltered the battered dreams of impoverished proprietors. Others had an aura of returning prosperity brought by their fields, now producing cane for a burgeoning sugar industry, and increasing river commerce. Bright new paint and formal gardens being rescued from encroaching subtropical growth proclaimed imminent prosperity. A fortunate few had never been diminished and gleamed brightly, even more now than before the years of horrible devastation. And there were still burned-out hulks thrusting skeletal chimney fingers at the night sky.

The planters, their blood often thinned by generations of disporting themselves in dissipations such as could only be found downriver in New Orleans fleshpots, shared a love of fine horseflesh, the best whiskeys, wines and liqueurs, and cigars. To possess

2

fast horses and faster women, they would kill in hot-blooded moments of fury, or with coldblooded concentration in the mists of dawn under a venerable oak. The women of the gentry were packaged in two varieties: the more interesting were the octoroon and Creole beauties whose tumultuous flesh was kept waiting in lavish but discreet apartments or houses with jalousied windows and ornate iron balconies in New Orleans; the second variety were the mistresses of the plantations, delicate creatures of fishbelly-white hue whose sole function was to be decorative while playing the role of gracious chatelaine. The capability to produce at least one male heir strong enough to live to maturity was also prized.

The proprietors were not to be confused, at least on the surface, with the Cajun.

The Cajun was an earthquake, a hurricane on two feet. The Cajun lived to sing, dance, fight, drink, and wench, and the more of these activities he could carry on at one time, the better he enjoyed his life.

A good number of the plantation owners also enjoyed most of these blood-stirring activities. They just hoped their wives, who were of course fully aware, would not become *publicly* aware, and thus be obliged to swoon, to cluck their elegant tongues when others were within earshot, and become screaming bitches in privacy, if such a thing as privacy could exist with a score of Negro house servants shuffling about in noiseless slippers.

The stretch of water where the rumpus took place was bordered on the west by Pointee Coupee Parish and on the east by West Feliciana Parish, many twisting river miles north of Baton Rouge. One notable

3

thing about it was that it broke out at almost the same instant in two areas of the *Dauphine* separated by social status, distance, and altitude: the teeming cargo deck and the promenade deck above, which had two classes of cabins and the dining room, saloon bar, and gambling pit. It didn't spread to the topmost Texas deck and its first-class staterooms and quarters for ranking officers and the master.

Oddly, the freight deck, teeming with roughnecks, was the scene of less serious physical damage than the promenade deck, where the passengers were, relatively speaking, gentry.

Below, there were lumps on heads, split lips, black eyes, some broken bones, and stabs and gouges; a few pistols were discharged. Above, there were broken bones, lost teeth, smashed faces, and fractured extremities; black eyes were parceled out wholesale. While no dead bodies were found, the sum total was more than disturbance of the peace. Some participants went over the side, and it was not known whether all these were alive at the time.

It erupted with the suddenness of a flash fire around Ki as he lounged on a stack of deck cargo near the bow of the packet. He was at peace, his golden-hued face reflecting the solemn repose of the Orient from which half his blood came. His dark eyes saw and his brain automatically calculated the activities of those around him, and there was nothing to alarm his senses. Deck passengers were doing the things deck passengers always did: whiling away the time until the next landing with cards and drinks under the soft light of oil lanterns, and in the shadowed areas indulging in various modes of sexual congress. Somewhere a harmonica warbled, a banjo tinkled, and a few Negroes were singing, the words of their tune a melodic but untranslatable stringing together of sounds.

Then came a shout, a curse, the smack of knuckles hammering flesh, and in seconds all hell had broken loose.

Ki got to his feet, clambered like a big cat to the highest convenient point, and waited to be entertained.

He guessed that some two dozen deck passengers became involved immediately, which would make about two out of three. The remainder delayed as much as a half-minute before opting to fight or flee. Most chose to join in.

Concern for Jessie made Ki glance toward the saloon deck, to see if the action was spreading that far up. His role in life called for him to be companion to, and protector of, the tall, long-limbed blonde and her worldwide business interests. But the tumult and shouting were not, as far as he could determine, going much beyond the lowbrows swarming around him.

Anyway, Jessie was quite capable of taking care of herself in such circumstances. Orphaned in her teens, growing up on several hundred thousand acres of prime Texas range, Jessica Starbuck was, by the time she took control of her immense fortune and its attendant responsibilities, as strong and capable as any human would ever have to be.

Fine-boned, aristocratic and proud-breasted, lithe-hipped, long-legged femininity notwithstanding, Jessie could be as tough as a keg of railroad spikes if need be.

Also, Ki reflected, she was in the company of Captain Gregory Thorpe, who towered several inches

5

over her, and had more bone, muscle, and sinew than most men would ever carry. He was master of the *Dauphine*—a solid, honest, working riverboat with predictable swiftness and passable amenities, particularly on the Texas deck, realm of the ship's officers and best-paying customers. Surely Captain Thorpe would keep trouble from the lady on his own boat.

Or so Ki believed.

He was not entirely correct in this assumption, as he was to learn in pretty short order.

At one of the gaming tables, Jessie was holding two high pair, and after some study of her fellow players, she had just about opted to draw one card and go for the full house. Her eyes, almost jade-green in the subdued lighting, had assessed the competition, and she guessed she was up against nothing more substantial than three of a kind going into the draw. She was sitting to the dealer's right. The thin, nervous man second from the dealer's left had been having poor luck, worse than no luck at all, but had opened for ten. And he had stayed after Jessie bumped it twenty to drive out the tourists, eliminating two and leaving five, including herself and the falsely jolly man who had dealt.

Nervous took two, virtually confirming the three-of-a-kind openers, and Jessie had a hunch she could bluff him out with the right raises, even if he improved to anything short of four of a kind. The man next to him was a pro, being hopeful with a high pair. Three there. Next was a beribboned woman who could not keep her ringleted head screwed on straight. Unfortunately, the nattering ninny was winning, and elected to play a pat hand.

The woman, in Jessie's opinion, either was gifted with dumb luck, was ahead because she was giving everyone else a splitting headache, or was a damn sly professional. Jessie was still trying to decide which it was, when a complete stranger flew over and crash-landed on the table.

The hand that was under way could never be reassembled. The table collapsed, scattering chips, hard coin, discards, drinks, cigars, and players—including Jessie. Whirling, trying to regain her balance, she noted peripherally that a stocky man, some fifteen feet away at the bar, was kissing his knuckles fondly.

Then the nattering lady screamed, close by her ear, "Hooliganism! The management shall hear of this outrage!"

"It just has," Jessie retorted, smoothing her skirt. "The management is fully aware, madam, and is acting."

The woman, her underskirts tumbled to show voluminous pantalettes, stared at Jessie's back. She had no comprehension of what Jessie had meant, no idea that the *Dauphine,* registered to the Havre Steam Navigation Company, was but one tiny fragment of the Starbuck holdings.

The steamboat firm had recently been plagued by a series of annoyances, some trivial, some serious to the point where boats, passengers, and cargoes had been in real danger. It was this troublesome situation that had brought Jessie and Ki to the Mississippi. And it was their intention, she had informed Captain Thorpe

7

when they boarded, to find a way to put a stop to it.

The captain had looked indignant, as though Jessie had insulted his ability to perform his duties properly.

"No disrespect to you, Captain," Jessie had quickly assured him. "Other shipping firms are having identical problems. Groundings at night because of navigation lights moved or tampered with, engines sabotaged, passengers harassed, cargo damaged or stolen. There are just too many rats swimming in this river, and from what we've heard, there's some organized intelligence well hidden in the background."

"I can't argue otherwise," Thorpe replied, his mouth grimly set above his wide jaw, his pale eyes smoldering with anger. "The Mississippi has more than its fair ration of riffraff." His massive hand angrily raked through his unruly thatch of brown hair, and his mustache, which he might have stolen from a cavalry trooper, had bristled with his anger. "Them as would usually be at each other's throats seem to have made some unholy peace and directed their attentions to robbing and pillaging honest men."

"For you, that's quite a speech, Gregory," Jessie commented. "Have you any workable ideas to counter future troubles?"

"A few, but they'd take their toll of the innocent as well as the guilty, I'm afraid," he ventured. "We can carry only so many crew. A platoon of Marines would be helpful."

"And impossible," Jessie responded. "So?"

"Some of the best brawlers from the New Orleans docks have been added to the crew. Men who know how to get to the heart of a fight and break heads," he said. "And two-inch fire hoses, each capable of

8

delivering five hundred gallons a minute, have been cut into the high-pressure engine room lines. They'll clear the decks like grapeshot, and the men have been trained in their handling."

"As the guilty go, so go the innocent," Ki put in.

"A last resort, but an effective one, I promise," Thorpe assured them.

And the voyage had thus far been without incident.

Now they had an incident.

And while Ki was calmly watching the melee on the lower deck, Jessie was taking a not-so-calm hand in the saloon.

She'd had high hopes of improving her two pair.

Chapter 2

The stocky man was built like a piano crate to which arms, legs, and a head had been attached—a piano crate that had been banged and scraped some during its journeys. The man's head was equally blocky, and it wore a pearl-gray derby. At this moment the most notable feature of the face was a wide mouth picketed with teeth, some gold, which were clamped tight to a fat cigar whose aroma proclaimed its worth at perhaps two and a half cents. The crate wore a checked suit and loud plaid vest, the uniform of a commercial traveler, a drummer.

Jessie marched toward him, eyes narrowed in anger, the slit skirt of her form-fitting suit flashing open to give lucky observers a glimpse of slender legs fitted into gleaming riding boots of soft black leather. Men made way for her, appreciating the high cheekbones and sultry mouth and the luxurious fall of copper-blond hair nearly to her waist.

With much of the bar all to himself, the crate waited. He winked a twinkling blue eye and spoke.

"Sorry, ma'am! Shamin' meself, I am, disturbin' a foine lady such as yerself! Me intent was only to show that Limey oaf the door, and the river beyond it, but the boat lurched, that not bein' any of me own doin' at all, ye see? 'Twas after puttin' me aim off, and the needed lift was not there, as ye've without doubt seen. Sure, and he'd of bounced a time or two on the deck before the splashin' and the drowndin' that's too good for the likes o' Her Majesty's sorry wretch!" He tipped the derby to Jessie, bowing. "'Tis yer pardon I'm after askin', ma'am, and that of yer company as well. Colin Deithe Moran, at yer service."

Jessie wasn't sure whether the brogue was real or stage Irish. But in this time and place, no one who was not Irish would claim to be so, which made it likely he was the genuine article. So she was about to drop the matter and let things smooth over when his foe ruined it.

"Mick swine! Whoreson Papist!"

The epithets came from behind her, and Jessie was rudely shoved aside by the flying man with the bloody nose, who was now in possession of a whiskey bottle. He was taller than the Irishman, and more tastefully dressed, if one overlooked the spreading stain on his shirt and suit caused by the blood gushing from his ruined nose. He swung the bottle at Moran's head, and in so doing knocked Jessie against the bar.

The Irishman, with a bellow of indignation, swung a hamlike fist from about the region of his knees. It

11

met the Englishman's face with the sound of a well-aimed bung starter. The impact sent the man reeling into the bystanders.

Some of the jostled spectators tried to grab the man's arms, while several others struck out at the Irishman, one wielding a leather-covered sap, which did nothing more than knock the Irishman's derby flying. The riled Irishman, having a neck in either hand, banged two heads together, and two unconscious men dropped at his feet. He reached out and got a grip on the sap, which its owner had made the mistake of more or less attaching to himself with a leather strap. It made a dandy handle with which to heave him over the bar. He brought down a rank of bottles, and knocked a keg of beer from its rack.

At this point, several frightened women began to scream loudly. The sound spurred more men to join in, many being total strangers who had nothing against one another.

Jessie somehow had her own island of space in which she stood, crouching, hands set the way Ki had trained her, ready to chop and slash and stab. She had a glimpse of Captain Gregory Thorpe elbowing in, shoving his way toward her, at the point of a flying wedge of burly sailors armed with pick handles, which were being put to good use in making people fall down. The accompanying din was awesome.

Jessie made her way unscathed through the turmoil to one of the big windows that opened above the lower decks. She poked her head out and, for the first time, became aware of the fisticuffs in progress below.

She spied Ki calmly watching from his vantage point atop a stack of cargo. The deck brawl looked

12

as though it wasn't going to amount to much. The *Dauphine* was continuing her steady downstream course, her pilot evidently inured to such goings-on.

Jessie leaned from the window, put two fingers between her lips, and let out a shrill whistle that caught Ki's attention.

"You're needed!" she shouted to him.

"Fine! Nothing much going on here!"

"Well, there is up here!"

She was jostled aside as a churning knot of battlers veered into the bulkhead beside her. She sprang back as three heaved a fourth from the window. Arms and legs windmilling, the man tumbled onto a stack of baled hides below.

Ki took off as if he had springs in his legs, heading for the saloon deck. Nobody tried to stop him.

Although nobody tried to stop him, Ki found it slow going on the two companionway ladders he was forced to use to reach the saloon deck. He was one of a throng that was becoming more tightly packed each moment, and it was as noisy as a raid on a Chinese gambling house. It seemed that everyone aboard the *Dauphine* had it uppermost in mind to go to another part of the boat immediately. Some clearly wanted to get away from the fighting, while others just as obviously wished to get to it.

In the pilothouse, a ship's officer was vigorously pulling the cord of the great steam whistle, and bells were jangling in the engine room belowdecks. There were intermittent splashes and cries of *"Man overboard!"* A cluster of sailors appeared with a firehose and began sluicing away. The jet of high-pressure water tumbled men and women alike.

13

Eventually a dripping Ki broke through the mob and into the saloon, where the better class of passengers was demonstrating that they could be just as rowdy and bloodthirsty as the steerage rabble. He spotted Jessie in the thick of the fray, defending herself with dexterous determination, her golden mane tossing as if caught in a whirlwind. And Ki knew that when it ended, and chaos simmered down to mere disorder, there would be hell to pay.

Ki began dodging hurtling bodies and casting others from his path, yet it took him nearly two minutes to reach Jessie's side. "What's the fight about?" he shouted.

"Politics. Watch out!"

A tall man with some of his clothes and most of an ear torn off was hurtling toward them. Ki pivoted, chopped him on the side of the neck, and moved Jessie aside as the man fell. Black eyes smoldering, Ki surveyed the turmoil for other attackers, and yelled in Jessie's ear, "We can't stay here, but down below isn't any better!"

"Quick! Other side of the bar—if we can make it!"

Ki grabbed her hand and broke for the bar, which was a natural line of both battle and sanctuary. Combatants were two and three deep along the mahogany, and piling up along the brass rail in various stages of damage. On the far side was comparative peace and quiet—and brawny bartenders, armed with bung starters and truncheons, clouting all those who would try to invade their calm territory.

With some well-placed kicks and chops, Ki gained them a place at the bar. One of the defenders lunged, swinging a pick handle. Ki caught his arm, twisted hard, and jerked the bartender's pained face close to his own.

"This is Jessica Starbuck! Help her over!"

The bartender was no help at all, his elbow having been dislocated, but he got out of the way and Jessie vaulted the bar with a none-too-gentle boost on the rump from Ki, who followed in an instant. They exchanged stares.

"I think we're the only two not hurt," she ventured.

"I wouldn't doubt it. Now what did you mean, politics?"

"An Irishman met an Englishman."

"Ah."

"What happened down below? When did *that* party begin?"

"Couple of minutes before you shouted from up here," Ki said. "No idea why. Maybe bad liquor and bad cards, or bad women."

"Or all three," Jessie mused. "Odd that both should break out at the same time."

"Yes," Ki agreed. "Worth talking about with Thorpe, when we can."

"Damn your eyes, belay it, all of you!"

Thorpe's quarterdeck bellow shook those paintings that hadn't already tumbled from the walls. He stood spraddle-legged atop the bar at the far end, a boat hook clenched in his fists, an eye beginning to purple. He was so tall he had to stoop beneath the overhead beams. He banged the boat hook loudly on the bar and shouted, *"Belay it, or it's over the side with the lot of you!"*

Almost immediately the battle royal diminished to

mere scuffling and cursing as the steamboat skipper prowled along the bar, occasionally taking a swipe at a handy head.

"I believe he has their attention," Jessie said.

"He has mine," Ki agreed as he surveyed the big room, which might have been the scene of a bear-baiting.

Everything in sight was destroyed or badly damaged. Recumbent human forms, at least three dozen of them, competed for deck space with the remains of tables, chairs, and the upright piano—which had been tumbled a good twenty feet from the small band stage. Shattered glasses, plates, spittoons, cards, dice, cushions, beer mugs, bottles of assorted spirits—virtually everything that had not been bolted down—were everywhere.

There was a lot of blood—a lot on people, more wherever people had been, and still more freshly dripping as walking wounded moved about, wearing glazed expressions. Through it all, Thorpe's bullyboys moved, prodding, poking with their pick handles for signs of life.

"Any dead here?" the captain called out.

His men continued their inspection, the one who was apparently their leader finally responding, "Guess not, Cap'n. Some as must wish they were. Lot of doctorin' needed."

At various points around the saloon and along the bar, those who were able to stand moved cautiously, assessing personal damage.

One raised his voice. "Jesus God, but I need a drink! How about it, Cap? Fight's over."

16

Thorpe considered this, then said, "All right. Belly up, those as still can."

Painfully, men and a few women made their way to the bar and reached for glasses of whiskey with shaking hands. Thorpe spotted Jessie and Ki, dropped down behind the bar, and approached them, biting a flap of skin from the bleeding knuckles of his right hand. "My God," he growled. "We really needed this! What set it off? Who—?"

"An Englishman and an Irishman met and *didn't* hit it off—so they hit each other," Jessie said. She rose on tiptoe and looked among the groaning bodies on the deck. After a minute she pointed to an unconscious man whose face looked like a burst tomato, adding, "I believe that's the Britisher, but it's hard to be certain, considering his condition." She continued to look around, slowly shaking her head. "But I don't see the Irishman or— *Yes!*" Her finger pointed accusingly at one of the barmen. With his jacket off, the derbied man who called himself Colin Deithe Moran was smiling around a fresh cigar and pouring beer and whiskeys for those who had made it to the bar. *"That* Irishman! That hulk with hardly a mark on him!"

"Aha!" Captain Gregory Thorpe said, speculating. "We will have words with him. He doesn't look damaged."

"He did enough damage," Jessie retorted. "And you didn't ask me if it was all right to serve drinks, Captain."

"Miss Starbuck, you are not the master of the *Dauphine*."

17

Ignoring the hot retort that was about to spring from her tongue, the captain strode down the duckboards behind the bar to where the Irishman was making a small joke as he poured liquor into the glass of a man who had a fat lip that drooped, and two teeth freshly gone. Thorpe got a glass of his own and held it out for filling. With no sign of repentance or discomfiture, the self-appointed barman poured.

"Ye're after bein' the master of this grand vessel," Moran ventured.

"Yes. I would like some words with you. I believe the owner would also." With a nod, Thorpe indicated Jessie, who was standing with Ki, watching.

"Oh Jesus—you're meanin' the grand lady there? We've met, in a manner of speakin'. I am Colin Deithe Moran, lately of County Cork. Me line is spirits."

"Come!"

"Ye're after havin' the mean speech of a bailiff," Moran responded, taking his time in filling a tumbler for himself before following to where Jessie and Ki waited. He tipped his hat respectfully, but then planted it firmly on his head as Thorpe completed the introductions. Then he said, "Miss Starbuck, I'd no mind to cause such destruction, no more than I meant to hit you with that sod as calls himself Thomas Sykes."

"Who's Sykes?"

"Captain, I believe that may be the gentleman Mr. Moran threw into the pot of the card game I was in," Jessie explained. "Mr. Moran intended to throw the man past us, I'm sure, through the door and overboard."

"That's it, Miss Starbuck," Moran said eagerly, and swept his hand around to indicate the other braw-

18

lers. "None of them was invited to the dance, and I'm not after taking the blame for all their bad manners."

"We know how it finished," Thorpe replied tersely. "Just how did it begin between you and Mr. Sykes?"

Moran shuffled his feet and took a long pull at his glass. "Well, sir, he made fun of me middle name, Deithe."

"Daisy?" Thorpe repeated in a fair approximation.

"To your ears, I suppose it must sound so. It's the Irish for David." He spoke slowly then. "Day-thee."

"Like 'daisy' with a lisp," Ki offered.

His genial face reddening, Moran retorted, "Whatever, the sod did call me Daisy, and I'd had more'n enough of his lip by then."

Thorpe looked suspicious. "You didn't provoke him?"

"By the Holy Virgin, sir, I was meself only after mindin' me own business, speculatin' on how I might speak to yourself, for a fact now, on the wisdom of consignin' the rotgut ye have behind the bar here and stockin' a fine line of spirits such as I'm offerin' to the quality trade."

"You don't seem to choke on our house whiskey," Thorpe retorted. "Get on with your story, man."

"Well, I was havin' a dram or two, and this Sykes feller—I'm knowin' him from New Orleans where he's employed as an embezzler for an import house— he was blatherin' on about what the English call the 'Irish problem,' which is some eight million of us as say seven hundred years of slavery to English landlords is not to our likin' at all. Well, he did not take note of an Irish problem not ten feet distant from his flappin' lip."

19

"So you threw him at some cardplayers," Thorpe cut in, hoping to shorten the account.

"Ah, but I spoke to him first."

"You did."

"Invited him to kiss me royal Irish, ah, arm."

"He declined, and *then* you hit him," Thorpe suggested.

"More or less, I did that." Moran's eyes shifted to Jessie. "Is it the Bridewell for meself, now?"

"Bridewell?"

"The hoosegow. Jail," Moran supplied.

The thought of tossing this miscreant into the brig had already passed through the captain's mind, but there were arguments against it. For one thing, he had no proper brig, and if he salted Moran away in the chain locker or some such place, it would mean keeping a crewman on guard continuously. The real problem might not be keeping Moran penned, but keeping others from him. The Irish were widely held, particularly in the deep South, to be no good whatsoever except for boozing, fighting, and lusting, and it was true that few had any of the skills held useful in this raw country. They were not artisans and craftsmen, as were the descendants of English yeomen, and for some reason knew less of farming than illiterate black field hands. Also, they were Catholics, and this was hardshell Baptist territory, despite the large numbers of French in Louisiana.

The *Dauphine*'s passenger manifest totaled nearly three hundred names. The captain estimated that no more than a third could possibly have been involved at all in this rumpus, and what went on down on the cargo deck was another matter indeed.

Yes, he thought, there was a strong possibility of a lynch mob forming. Moran was clearly a man who could take care of himself. Thorpe said, "Not if you behave."

Moran tried for a tone of deep sincerity when he said, "I've made me apologies and will give no trouble, sir."

"Fair enough," Thorpe agreed, and waved a sailor over. "Fetch the purser with the passenger roster. I want a head count. And pass the word that anyone claiming to be a doctor is wanted here immediately, and then go ask the pilot if we're still on the river or in some fool bayou!"

"The lawyers are going to eat well on this for a long time," Jessie predicted. "I suppose we might as well have a drink ourselves, while we can still enjoy one."

"Sure, and that will make everything right," Moran noted, moving to bring glasses and a bottle, pouring, and then adding, "Or surely lead us to believe so."

Jessie sighed, and from the corner of his mouth, Ki murmured to her, "I think *we* may have an Irish problem."

Chapter 3

Before fifteen minutes had passed, the saloon became an anthill of activity. Five men who claimed to be doctors of one shade or another were stitching and splinting and taping, aided by several women who knew about patching up men. Three of these were prostitutes bound for New Orleans. The purser was making a body count throughout every section of the *Dauphine*, while crewmen were clearing away the debris, throwing most of it over the side.

Ki and Jessie moved around and through it, making their private assessments of what had happened and how well it was being handled. Very well, they judged; Captain Thorpe had parceled out tasks and responsibilities, and was firmly making sure they were tended to correctly.

"Between us," Jessie commented, "I think we've

tended about as many wounds as we're looking at now."

Ki nodded. "But it's odd, Jessie. The scrap down on the cargo deck didn't leave half as many injured as there are up here."

"Third-class passengers are used to pounding on one another," Jessie replied, "but I remember hearing the captain mention that fact to the first mate, too."

"And don't ask me what set it off down there. No threats or arguing, just suddenly there it was. I almost felt it would turn itself off when it got ready. Maybe it's the muggy weather, or the strange smells hereabouts."

"Speaking of strange things, where's Sykes?"

"Thorpe had him moved to a stateroom on the Texas deck. He got the best doctor aboard to piece his face back together."

"Well, at least he's where Mr. Moran won't get at him again. Which brings us around to the other strange thing. I've got a funny feeling like yours, Ki, only mine is that our jolly Irishman didn't take this trip just to sell whiskey to Thorpe, but— Never mind, here come both men now."

Approaching with the Irishman in tow, Thorpe gestured that he wanted to see them, and then he said, "Could we all go topside, please?"

He led the way. His quarters occupied the forward stateroom on the starboard side of the Texas deck, and had access to corresponding space on the port side, which was the domain of the ship's officers, the first and second mates, the chief engineer, the pilots and visiting top brass. A sloping companion ladder led to the wheelhouse perched above. Jessie had been

23

assigned to the stateroom immediately behind Thorpe's cabin. In ranks of two abreast, entered from the promenades on either side, were eighteen more staterooms running aft. Passengers accommodated in them paid high rates for the privilege of being transported in the greatest luxury the *Dauphine* had to offer. Often, a majority of these rooms were occupied by gamblers or ladies of pleasure, who considered the added cost a necessary business expense.

Gregory Thorpe being a large man, he had a suitably large bed, and on most trips he was visited there by the ladies of pleasure, a diversion that he eschewed on this voyage, what with Jessica Starbuck herself right next door. They did not know each other well, having met face to face only a few times, chiefly at gatherings of the Board of Directors of the Havre Steam Navigation Company. Although only in his mid-thirties, Thorpe was a senior captain of the line and a member of the board.

Beyond the bed, the master's cabin was furnished with a desk, a fold-down chart table, a wardrobe, a chest of drawers, a brass-cased chronograph, a barometer and a compass, several undistinguished paintings and lithographs, a liquor cabinet, a mirrored washstand, and three comfortable chairs. A speaking tube made it possible from here to shout orders and maledictions to various parts of his vessel, but he seldom used it. He didn't need mechanical aids to make himself heard.

An officer in a neat blue uniform, with two braided stripes on his sleeve cuffs, had been sitting in a chair, going through a sheaf of papers and a notebook. He rose respectfully as they entered, a man of medium height and slender build, approaching middle age. Salt-and-pepper hair framed a lean, deeply tanned face of which a forward-thrusting lantern jaw was the most prominent feature. Thorpe introduced him as Leon LaFlemme, the first officer.

"What have you to report?" Thorpe asked La-Flemme, as he gestured to the others to sit where they pleased.

The first officer consulted his notebook. "Total injuries, of which only two were crew, seventy-three so far. Of these, only a score require more than first aid for cuts, bruises, and so forth, and should be put ashore at Baton Rouge for hospitalization. The most serious case is a Mr. Sykes. A possible skull fracture, broken nose, broken jaw, is missing nine teeth and'll lose more."

"Evidently no lives lost, which is the only pleasant surprise of the night," Thorpe growled. "I heard the usual 'man overboards,' so how many are we short?"

The officer swallowed hard. "However many absconded, we have nineteen more than we should."

"Blasted stowaways!" Thorpe slammed a fist into an open palm. "These boats ride so low, they can just swim out from shore and board us. I've a mind to build a great steel cage, and broil every one of 'em we catch!"

"We do what we can," LaFlemme pleaded. "Now, as to damage to the *Dauphine* herself . . ." He gave a recital of carnage in the saloon—a good thousand dollars' worth—but there was no structural damage to the vessel itself, and the fighting on the freight deck

25

had not penetrated to the engine room or the paddle-wheel and its driving mechanism. "We were lucky, sir," he concluded.

"Well, we could have come off a lot worse," Thorpe growled. "Looks like those high-pressure hoses broke up the mischief on the cargo deck before it got started good. And that team of dock-wallopers we signed on knew just what to do when they followed me into the saloon. Cut that brawl down in short order, even though we'd never figured on anything like it up there. The line's agents can worry about the damage claims. My intent now is to get to Baton Rouge in good time. I hope we don't have too many unscheduled landings."

"There's a point I'd like to make, Captain," the first officer said with some hesitation. "Might Mr. Moran be interested in seeing the river from a place few passengers are invited to visit? I mean, the pilot-house above us?"

"If you have in mind the steam launches as was astern of us, I was after takin' note of them meself," the Irishman replied, making no move to leave and casting a questioning glance at Thorpe. "Four launches, and a load of men in each, Captain, quarter to a half-mile astern, mixin' in with other craft. Too far to make out much about the lot aboard 'em before dark fell."

"I was aware of them early on, Mr. Moran," Thorpe replied, "and recall nothing unusual about them. There are hundreds of such craft on the water at any time, shuttling from shore to shore and landing to landing."

"And when might ye have last had reason to look 'em over before the sport began?"

Thorpe paused, then said, "About dusk was the last

I had business in the pilothouse. After that I was at my paperwork here, or on the saloon deck with routine duties."

"Then ye'd not have seen those flatboats the Cajuns use—pirogues or whatever they may be called—which came from shore and tied on to the launches?"

"I didn't."

"I did, sir, and Mr. Moran is right. That's what I was going to bring up. I didn't like the look of them."

"I've heard of river pirates, and I know nothing of their ways of plyin' their trade," Moran declared. "But with the English duties what they are, the Irish are keen smugglers, deft in furtive moves on the water. I'd be after imaginin' pirates would be similar."

"And how did you happen to take note of them, Mr. Moran?" Thorpe demanded.

"Ah, well, bein' a peaceful man meself, I stood apart at the bar, overhearin' the blatherin' of Sykes, and felt I owed it to meself and society to take a stroll on deck and ponder the virtues of keepin' the peace over givin' him the chastisement he was after seekin', sir. It was then I took note of the activities astern."

"Obviously, chastisement won out," Thorpe commented. "I will have to ask around about this."

"Just what are we talking about here, Captain?" Jessie inquired. "It sounds like the sort of trouble that brought me here."

"Oh, there's more pirating every season, Miss Starbuck," Thorpe replied, "but it's been relatively petty stuff, hit-or-miss small bands. Creoles, renegade Indians, whites, all colors. No threat to a vessel the size and speed of the *Dauphine* on the water. They've been limited to pirogues and flat-bottom skiffs that can

27

vanish into the bayous in minutes. Now, if somehow they've gotten financing for steam launches, it could be a different story. But there've been no reports of such attacks."

"There's always a first time," Ki said.

"Do you have enough crew to operate the *Dauphine* and still fight off a sizable band, or are we looking at a real danger?" Jessie pressed.

"You saw how fast my men stopped the trouble aboard—not more than ten minutes after going into action," Thorpe replied curtly. "And they were up against a good-sized mob. A really rough boarding party, men who know their business, might be different if there were enough of them. But no piddling steam launch is going to come close to the knots we can make."

"Has the *Dauphine* ever been raced, Captain Thorpe?" Jessie inquired with deceptive sweetness. Match races between riverboats were commonplace, with large sums wagered, but they were against all official company policies because of the danger and wear and tear to the craft involved.

"We're not talking of racing here," the master said noncommittally. "We're talking about piddling launches."

"Of course," Jessie agreed, rolling her eyes, and decided this was not the time to pursue the matter of sub rosa speed contests. "I can see we have a continuing pestilence on the Mississippi, and—

A rumbling *whuuuummmmp!* that might have been a mortar shell shook the *Dauphine* from stem to stern at that instant, and the deck beneath their feet trembled.

28

"Damn it to hell!" the captain shouted. "Boilers!"

He rocketed from the stateroom, while LaFlemme jumped for the ladder and scuttled up to the pilothouse, calling for bell signals to stop engines and muster fire and damage-control parties, then dropped down again, nearly bowling Jessie and Ki over as he followed Thorpe. The two officers did not bother with the companion ladders, but pounded down the Texas deck promenades to their farthest point aft, and there heaved lines that snaked over the saloon deck to the cargo level and provided a fast, if dangerous, route to the boiler and engine rooms.

The mighty steam whistle added its bellow to the clamor of bells and rising shouts of alarm from the passengers. The doors of the staterooms on the Texas deck were flying open, and passengers in varying stages of undress rushed out, making for the companionways to the lower decks.

Jessie, Ki, and Moran, swiftly recovering from stunned surprise, ran behind the captain and the first mate. They sensed that valuable time might be wasted trying to battle their way through the swelling mob of frightened passengers, and elected to take the rope route. Losing little elegance or dignity despite the flaring of her skirt, Jessie was only seconds behind Thorpe on one line, and Ki matched her speed on the second. She glanced up in time to see Moran hurriedly making the sign of the cross before following. All five held fast to the hemp lines, their feet barely bouncing on the lower promenade before they went over the rail and fetched up hard on the rocking cargo deck, a few feet above the river's surging waterline.

Through it all, the *Dauphine,* the rotation of her

massive paddles slowing, seemed to be keeping an even pace. There had been only the single blast, and no flames were visible as uniformed crewmen bearing axes and pry bars, and dragging firehoses, bowled over huddling passengers en route to a door that hung askew on its hinges. Out of the door drifted clouds of thin, noxious smoke.

Being the owner of the *Dauphine* didn't save Jessie from almost being knocked flat by a giant sailor who was running interference for the hose team.

"Outta the way, you muckers!" the brute roared, and gratuitously slammed an ax handle into Moran's ribcage while passing. Moran folded, wheezing, unable to do more than croak vile Irish retribution upon the man. Ki had the wit to get out of the way while the getting was good and leave the crew space to do its job. As Moran struggled upright, Ki pushed Jessie and him back against the rail, and not a moment too soon.

Seconds after the men ran into the smoke, huge chunks of wood, some over six inches thick and five feet long, began flying through the doorway, high over the rail, to splash into the murky, dark waters. A cordon of deckhands, arms linked, was holding back a mob of curious passengers. The air was enriched by curses in English, Spanish, and French. Several minutes passed before the barrage of firewood ceased and a dozen begrimed men emerged, a few of them being helped by their comrades.

"All right, all right, back to what you were about! No danger now!" one bellowed repeatedly. "Go back!"

Only by his face did they recognize the captain, who was as black from head to foot as any stoker.

His huge chest heaved as he gulped in fresh air. When he saw the trio, he wiped grime from his eyes and stalked over to them. They saw that he was not only blackened, but sopping wet.

"What was it?" Jessie demanded.

"Go back to my quarters, Miss Starbuck. All of you, in fact. I'll be along as soon's I scrub this soot off me."

"Was it pirates? Sabotage?" Jessie persisted.

"Dynamite planted in the woodpile. Now, dammit, woman, get topside!" He pivoted on his heel and stomped through the thinning spectators without a backward glance.

Jessie glared at the retreating figure, then turned indignantly to the others. "You heard him! Upstairs!"

"Topside," Ki corrected.

Moran fished a flask from his pocket, took a quick nip, and followed, grinning.

Chapter 4

They cooled their heels for more than an hour in Thorpe's quarters, with no break in the monotony except for a brief visit from a steward, who came to fetch a clean uniform from the wardrobe. The *Dauphine* was under way again, and from the wheelhouse above, the pilot assured them the vessel was answering the helm normally and the engines were responding, though with reduced power.

When Thorpe finally arrived, he was again immaculately dressed and a cigar was clamped jauntily between his fine teeth. He acknowledged the presence of his guests with a curt nod, went to the small bar, poured four fingers of bourbon into a tumbler, drank half of it off, then pulled the cigar from his mouth and barked, "Well, we *were* lucky with that one— and it *was* sabotage! Chunk of firewood that somebody'd improved by burying a stick of dynamite in it."

"And it exploded in the boilers?" Jessie asked.

"No, thank God." Thorpe took a deep breath and another drink from his glass. "If it had gone into the firebox, both boilers would've burst under hundreds of pounds of steam pressure, and the *Dauphine* would've been blown straight to hell." He sank wearily to his desk, continuing, "Instead, a stoker dropped the log on the deck, hard enough to spark off the dynamite. They're still collecting bits of two stokers and an assistant engineer from the bulkheads and overhead down there."

"Lord," Jessie murmured, shocked. "Couldn't there be more explosives hidden—"

"Not now," Thorpe interrupted. "Every stick of pitch pine and oak aboard went over the side. That leaves me with nothing to burn but what's in the firebox now, and it won't last me much longer than an hour."

"Fine kettle o' fish," Moran declared. "Wood is to be had close by these parts, I'm hoping?"

"Fuel landings every few miles," Thorpe assured them. "What we need to find is one that has dry oak. The stacks are caked thick with creosote from the pine. We'll take on just enough to make Baton Rouge tomorrow, where we'll tie up for repairs. That could take a while."

"A couple of days?" Ki ventured.

"Make that a couple of *weeks,* if we have to go into the tubes."

Jessie frowned. "Can we afford such a major delay? You've a full load of freight that isn't going to *swim* south, and the passengers have enough to complain about already."

"The *Dauphine*'s sister ship, the *Evangeline,* is at Baton Rouge, just fitted with new paddle frames and not yet back on the shipping roster. We'll borrow her from Cap'n Fitz."

Jessie's frown turned to a mirthless smile. "Just that simple, is it? You'll stroll onto Captain Jimmie Fitzhugh's bridge, and wrest his command from him?"

"By the time we tie up at Baton Rouge, I'll have thought up a diplomatic approach to handle Cap'n Fitz."

"It could require more than diplomacy," Jessie warned, her smile now growing cagey, though her voice became demure. "Of course, if you need help, a little persuasive influence—"

"I am sure I shall not require your services, dear lady," Thorpe retorted stoutly. "I can handle any matter involving Cap'n Fitz myself, as befitting equal officers and gentlemen." He raised his glass and drained it. "But for the moment I have a vessel to command, and a few items wanting attention. Perhaps you'd all care to retire and clean up?"

"I would certainly like to find someplace less stuffy," Jessie replied. With that, she gathered her skirts about her and marched from Thorpe's quarters, closely followed by Ki and Moran, both of whom were careful to keep their faces absolutely straight.

When they came to her stateroom, Jessie said, "I think I will wash and change." She opened the door, and turned to Moran. "Perhaps I shall see you later, Mr. Moran."

Moran doffed his derby. "I trust so, Miss Starbuck.

I'll be in the saloon, if ye should feel like chattin'."

Then, with a nod to Ki, Jessie went in and closed the door. The two men went as far as the next stateroom, which was Ki's. There they parted, Ki going inside while Moran continued on to parts unknown.

Ki set a match to his room's bracket lamp. Golden light suffused the small yet elegantly furnished interior, and thanks to the *Dauphine*'s pressure system, running water was piped directly to its marble washstand. While he was filling the basin, he noticed that the connecting door was open a bit, so he called, "Do you want to talk, Jessie?"

From the adjoining stateroom came the sound of a boot being thrown to the floor. Smiling wryly, Ki removed his suit jacket, sky-blue shirt, and string tie, leaving him only in his trousers and black ankle-high boots. He began to wash.

"Ki?"

"Mm."

Again there was a long stretch of silence.

Ki didn't press it. He dumped the soapy water, ran fresh and rinsed himself off, then went to the wardrobe for a clean shirt. He didn't really want to go out in his suit again; he would have preferred to change into his customary work clothes, which were more comfortable but hardly proper for this sort of occasion. Yet, on second thought, the occasion had turned out to be anything but formal; it had become dirty, mean, and deadly in very short order, and every instinct was warning him it could get worse before the trip was over.

So Ki stripped completely, and quickly donned what appeared to be plain, simple range garb: faded

35

jeans, a loose-fitting, collarless shirt, and a worn leather vest. But instead of boots, he slipped on Asian-style rope-soled cloth slippers; and instead of a regular belt, he wrapped his waistband twice around with a rope from which, at each end, steel weights dangled, and in his vest pockets he stashed a supply of *shuriken*, little razor-sharp steel disks shaped like six-pointed stars. Into his waistband he thrust the lacquered sheath containing his short, curve-bladed *tanto*.

He'd just finished rigging his vest when the connecting door swung all the way open, and Jessie stood on the threshold.

"Good idea," she said, noting his clothes.

"Perhaps, but I hope I'm overdoing it."

"I do too, Ki, I do too. Do you think I should—?"

He shook his head. "No, you'd better stick with your buttons and bows, Jessie. You're a Starbuck, *the* Starbuck and the owner besides, and that's the image you should show."

"I know, you're right. I was just hoping you'd talk me out of it." Then, crossly, she added, "And I just wish Captain Thorpe would stop holding it against me."

Ki gave her one of his inscrutable smiles, and wisely said nothing. But he was thinking that if the good Captain Thorpe happened to see Jessica now, he'd be wanting to hold himself against her, and to hell with her being his boss.

Jessie had changed out of her soiled outfit, but hadn't yet changed into anything else. All she was wearing was a tiny set of step-ins that would have been appropriate for a lady of the evening. And when she'd mentioned Thorpe just now, she'd given a kind

36

of angry shrug, making her full, firm breasts quiver, and her wealth of unpinned, coppery blond hair flow across her shoulders. Very erotic.

But not for him. On the rare moments when Ki saw her unclad like this, he knew that deep down it was a great compliment, that Jessie considered him her total friend, the one person she could trust to the grave. To have it otherwise, to be lovers, would have made the relationship they now had impossible.

And Jessie, he knew, was funny about sex. Her desire for it seemed to be something she could turn on or off at will. For months she would sleep alone, and then circumstances would place her in close proximity to a certain man, and the result of their joining would be on the order of a dreadnaught battleship's ammunition magazine exploding.

Ki sensed the signs; he sensed that it was inevitable that sooner or later, likely sooner, Captain Gregory Thorpe would also see Jessie like this.

"I don't know who's more irritating," Jessie continued. "The blarneying Mr. Moran, or our stiff-necked skipper."

"Give Thorpe his due. He's a proud man."

"Who thinks I'm only a silly female who should be house-bound, instead of invading his man's domain."

"The boat's his domain, and I suspect he'd resent anyone, man or woman, young or old, who intruded, friendly and well-meaning or not. Especially when things are going badly for him."

Some of the temper left Jessie then, and she allowed, "Oh, I know that's right as well as you do. Don't mind me, I just had my back up, that's all."

37

She laughed then, lightly, as if at herself. "And Mr. Moran? Shall we give him his due?"

Ki shrugged. "If we find out who he is."

"So we agree. He isn't what he hopes we think he is."

"Shall we take him up on his offer?"

"Ki, I believe I feel a spell of chatting coming on," Jessie said as she edged back and began closing the door. "Wait while I slip into something more uncomfortable."

Minutes later, Ki escorted Jessie down to the saloon. She moved with lithe, regal grace in the tailored moire waistcoat and skirt of a stylish castor-colored ensemble—although from the glances she kept giving Ki, it was apparent that she would have traded it gladly for her jeans and matching denim jacket.

Officially, the bar had been closed while its staff and the crew shoveled up the wreckage and arranged whatever was left unbroken. Yet it came as no surprise to them to discover that Moran had managed to talk his way inside. In addition, he'd managed somehow to lay hands on a full quart of real French cognac, and had cornered the head barman, to whom he was trying to sell a huge order of spirits.

"You gotta clear it with Cap'n Thorpe, Mr. Moran, and he's got more'n booze on his mind right now," the bar manager said, standing quickly with relief as Jessie and Ki appeared. "Evening. I'll bring more glasses."

The three settled at one of the remaining tables, and when the glasses came, Moran filled them, toasting: "Here's to the health of the walking wounded. What can go wrong next?"

"Let's talk about what's happened already," Jessie replied. "A whiskey drummer is bound to be a well-traveled man—one who notices things others might miss."

"Like odd boats in our wake? As I said, I was merely after takin' a stroll to cool down, and lo, there they were," Moran explained, eyeing her over the rim of his glass.

"Captain Thorpe saw them too, but he didn't feel they were important," Jessie said. "And he's no fool."

"And no doubt his judgment was the right one, for they've not come nigh, have they now?"

"Forgive me, Mr. Moran, if I don't entirely believe what you've been presenting. True, the trouble did start on board, and the log with the dynamite in it was loaded somewhere upstream, perhaps not even on this trip. But what if those *were* pirates back there, waiting for that log to be used? The *Dauphine* would have been lost, and many lives with it."

"True, Miss Starbuck. And 'tis true I'm an observant man, although observin' and deducin' are not one and the same."

"Possibly not, Mr. Moran, though in your case I doubt you're often wrong in what you think you see. And I'm interested in what you might've seen, other than those boats."

Moran sipped his cognac slowly, contemplatively. Finally he said, "Very well. F'rinstance, do you recall, during your game, a player who looked to be half pimp, half river gambler?"

Jessie thought back, and nodded. "The man was staying about even. Talked little, most likely because that impossible fat woman never shut up."

39

"But kept winning," Moran filled in. "She's known as Minnie the Mouth around New Orleans, and she's partners with the man. René Duvin, by name. He's what I said, a pimp and gambler with connections in high places. Call it and he's done it—opium, gun running, white slaving—and whenever he's arrested, he's always sprung in a shake. Maybe seeing Duvin and then them launches chuffing along behind us led me to an unwarranted conclusion, but . . ."

His voice trailed off. Ki said, "I got to the fight late, but didn't see anyone like that in it."

"Duvin's not after stayin' where his brain could be righteously bashed in," Moran said. "Indeed, he was scuttlin' for the door the instant ol' Sykes hit the table."

"I'm also interested in Sykes." Jessie's eyes studied Moran intently. "Granted, your people have reason to hate the English, but there was more than that involved. When you hit Sykes, it was personal. You meant to kill him."

"If, as ye think, Miss Starbuck, it was personal, then it's 'tween me and Sykes, and not for discussin'. Right?"

"You've already been discussing him," Jessie insisted. "When you were explaining your part in the riot to Captain Thorpe, you described Sykes as 'an embezzler for a New Orleans import house,' or some such thing."

"Lord spare me from persistent ladies," Moran muttered. He returned her stare, saying at last, "The 'some such thing' is more on the mark. Sykes juggles the books for a factoring firm, Continental Express Forwarders, in New Orleans. A grand cover for whatever he really does. All I know for certain is that he's an agent for foreigners."

"An English spy?" Ki asked.

"Not a-tall. That's one point I'm sure of. He isn't working here for the English," Moran said firmly, drinking deeply. "I know, 'cause I work for the English."

If Moran had intended to stun his two listeners, he had succeeded. They gaped at him.

"It follows along with war making strange bedfellows," he elaborated. "I'll keep it simple, but attend me words. For centuries the English have occupied Ireland, and all the while, it's our buckos who fill the ranks of their armies, raisin' the Union Jack to earn a few quid and keep their families from total starvation. Are ye followin' me?"

Jessie and Ki nodded.

"Now England has enemies, strong enemies, the most notable bein' France and Germany. One or t' other or both are forever plotting a way across the Channel. And there, on England's left flank, lies poor Ireland; a halfway smart invasion launched at the same time across the Channel and the Irish Sea would slay us along with the bloody lion."

"So the devil you know is better than one you don't."

"Exactly, Ki. No point in exchangin' the English, of whom we'll rid ourselves eventually, for armies of Frogs or Prussians. Or God only knows who else."

"What's that last bit mean?" Jessie asked.

"Just what I'm after sayin' to ye," Moran went on. "Some power—and it mayn't even be an organized government—has been providin' our Fenian movement with guns and money, all of which we need in a way ye can't imagine."

"America? Is it coming from here?"

"A large portion, to be sure. You must know of the millions who've come here since the famines of the thirties. There's none without family left behind, and dreams of home. So there are hundreds of thousands of ready-made contacts here with the bitterest folk ever put on God's earth."

Jessie and Ki locked eyes, nodding with an understanding Moran could not fathom. Jessie said softly, "The cartel."

"Cartel? Which cartel? Cartels abound these days."

"Mr. Moran, you've undoubtedly heard of the Starbuck enterprises. They're worldwide, with resources greater than those of many countries. Well, I own every bit of it."

"Aye, you are famous. But what of this cartel?"

"It too spans the globe, and is surely larger than Starbuck, which it wants to destroy. The feeling is mutual. Anyway, its leadership is European-based, mostly Germans, although our attempts to pin it down specifically have so far not accomplished much. It's seemingly everywhere, yet nowhere, corrupting and manipulating commerce, finance, politics, whatever and however it can. We know it seeks to control the United States, but its ultimate goal could well be world domination."

"And y'say it's wantin' to destroy you?"

Jessie took a long swallow of cognac. "It killed my mother, Sarah Starbuck, when I was a baby. Then, after my father, Alex, began a personal campaign against it, the cartel kept trying to murder him too. It finally succeeded. I'm continuing the fight. So is it. It has no morals, obeys no laws. It is cunning, vicious, and ruthless, and believe me, it very much exists. It *must* be stopped."

"I believe you. The sound of it has a familiar ring . . ." Moran didn't elaborate, but sat tapping his fingers for a moment before asking, "By chance, now, would a member of this cartel be a tall, white-haired Prussian? In his mid-thirties, maybe, with an artificial left hand of steel?"

Ki stiffened. "Von Eismann!"

"Yes, we knew the man," Jessie explained. "To us, he was the Iceman, one of the cartel's top lieutenants and assassins, and he specialized in murdering by hand, his mechanical hand. But Von Eismann's dead now. Ki killed him. Why do you ask?"

"I'd heard rumors of such a devil, though only once from one who'd actually encountered him." Moran's voice became grim. "A chum of mine he was, a trusted compatriot, but I fear an innocent. I later found him with his head crushed as if by a vise, 'cept for the fact of fingermarks in his skull. So, Ki, tell me, are you positive Von Eismann's dead?"

"He is dead." Ki spoke softly, and his eyes were like black onyx. "He has to be dead. I killed the Iceman twice, as dead as any man could be. Your devil has gone to hell, where he belongs."

"Faith, and here comes the captain," Moran declared, abruptly hearty as he caught sight of Thorpe striding toward them. "And don't he have the look of the devil in his eye!"

Thorpe picked up a glass on the way, sat down at the table, and poured himself a drink. "We are making

43

a landing to take on wood in a quarter-hour," he announced. "With the help of the Lord and a fine current, we won't have to break out oars and row the last mile."

This cheered everyone, although Jessie was prompted to ask, "What of the steam launches that were trailing us?"

"Nary a sign of 'em. They probably turned back. Or they might've easily slid past us while we were dealing with the boiler room. In any case, I hope it'll set your mind at ease about those boats, Miss Starbuck, when you learn that I've come up with a guaranteed nasty surprise for anyone who tries to board us."

"And what might that be?" Moran inquired.

Thorpe merely smiled craftily and replied, "I'd prefer not to go into details, for security's sake."

Jessie felt a sneaking suspicion that it was also for Captain Thorpe's sake, should the faint-hearted feminine owner of the steamboat pull rank and forbid his scheme.

"Let me just say," Thorpe added, "that if we have uninvited guests, stand well clear of the firehoses. *Well* clear, someplace like the Texas promenade deck."

A series of short, sharp blasts on the whistle and the clamoring of engine-room bells brought Thorpe to his feet. He left as the *Dauphine* shuddered to a halt. Within minutes, crewmen could be heard shouting on the freight deck as the gangplanks were lowered and the sternwheeler was made fast, ready to take on the much-needed fuel.

44

Chapter 5

"Let's watch this from up above," Ki suggested.

Carrying their glasses, the three climbed to the Texas deck, where they surveyed the scene below, lit by ship lanterns and bonfires on shore.

"He's taught 'em to move right spritely," Moran commented. "You have to give the captain that."

Already crewmen were teeming on and off the gangplanks, muscling heavy dollies of split logs aboard and storing them in the bunker. Their straining features glistened with sweat, but they never let up under the hawkish eyes and steady orders of the petty officers. Sparks blasted upward from the huge twin funnels that rose high above the pilothouse, as fresh fuel was heaved into the red maws of the fireboxes far below. And soot rained down everywhere.

"He's guarding them right well, too," Ki noted.

Armed with shotguns or carbines and holstered sidearms, other crewmen were standing fore and aft of the *Dauphine,* as well as along the bank and at either end of the gangplanks. Thorpe himself could be seen leaning from the pilothouse window, a rifle crooked in his arm, and his eyes scanning in all directions.

Even so, he somehow missed them when they came.

The first that Jessie, Ki, and Moran knew of the boarders was an exchange of gunfire on the riverward side of the boat, and a sudden shouting below them on the water. At that moment they could not see just what was happening, because the overhang of the saloon deck canopy blocked their view. The whistle sounded urgently, and they had a glimpse of Thorpe leaping from the pilothouse to the Texas promenade, clutching his rifle, a sheathed saber slapping against his thigh. Landing, Thorpe caught his balance with agility before running past them toward the disturbance.

"Come with us!" Jessie called, grabbing Moran and tugging him along as she and Ki bolted for her stateroom.

Once inside, she threw open the lid of a trunk, disclosing a couple of Winchester .44-40 carbines and a couple of Colt Frontier revolvers chambered for the same rounds, of which there were extra boxes aplenty.

"When you know there's been trouble, it pays to be prepared for more," she explained hastily, tossing a carbine and a pistol to the startled Irishman. "Know how to use these?"

"Do I!" He stuffed spare ammunition into his pockets, and pounded with surprising speed around to the portside.

Thorpe had already taken up a position there, and was firing his rifle into a flatboat drifting close by the *Dauphine*. Several shapes, two of them moving weakly and the rest sprawled motionless, were in the small craft.

"Spread out! Cover the bow and stern! Anything in the water, shoot it!" Thorpe yelled as he took careful aim at a swimming figure. He fired, and the figure disappeared beneath the surface.

Moran laughed. "Good eye, sir!"

Ki, who seldom used firearms, took a position in the bow. Jessie hunkered down midway between Thorpe and Moran, who was pouring a selective and effective hail of lead astern.

The air reverberated with the mingled roars of the whistle and the weaponry. Flame-lanced bullets seared the night with deadly precision, splintering wood and tearing through flesh and bone.

Moran tilted his derby the better to sight on a launch hovering some fifty yards astern. He squeezed off three rapid rounds, and as if shot point-blank, each found its mark, sending the rest of the launch's crew diving over the side.

"And it's a grand night for the Irish Navy!" Moran bellowed as he began systematically to pick off the pirates now floundering in the water.

His words were lost as two separate screaming sounds arose from the region of the freight deck, and along with them a billowing cloud of steam, which was quickly joined by a second and third.

"Lay it on 'em good, men!" Thorpe bellowed, and began firing at fresh targets, men swimming in panic away from the hull of the *Dauphine*. "Cook their mis'rable sausages!"

Amid the rising steam, fusillades of rifle and pistol fire continued to rake the water. Oddly, throughout it all, the loading gang continued its labors, protected by the deadly curtain of bullets.

Thorpe shouted his best for a full two minutes before the shooting stopped and relative quiet returned. The steam whistle and the odd, steady screeching sound that had risen from the cargo deck became silent. Then there was only the screaming of men and their moaning, pitiful cries, now being overlaid by a rising hubbub of bellowed questions and answers and orders to do one thing or stop doing another.

Grinning in triumph, Captain Thorpe led his group of defenders below, pushing a path through babbling passengers, all of whom seemed to want his immediate attention at once.

He sought out the bosun, a light-skinned black man the size and heft of a draft horse, big enough to dwarf both Thorpe and the solid Moran together. "What was it, Boats? How'd we do?"

"Jes' river scum, Cap'n Thorpe, suh," the bosun reported. "Small boats like you warned us, but the first 'uns got over the railin' quick afore we spot 'em. Then we bust heads an' give 'em the steam like you said. Shore cooked they gooses good! Yeah!"

"How many?"

"Hard to say, Cap'n, suh. Mebbe twelve to twenty git aboard. We got none of 'em dead here, shot, cut, an' scalded. Must be that many more didn' make it

48

this far. I'm meanin' they got here but left dead, you know? Not countin' them as you folks shot from topside, or blowed to hell!"

"All dead? Damn! Wish there was one or two left alive to question," Thorpe said. "Well, dump the meat over the side. Let the river have them."

"Mebbe, suh, if you was to send a party ashore, there'd be some wounded you could catch," the bosun offered. "Mah boys jes' get goin' good!"

Thorpe considered it, then said, "No time. These were just footsoldiers anyway. The men who hired them are likely sippin' drinks in some fancy house in Baton Rouge or New Orleans." He glanced at a body draped over the rail. Half-breed Creole. "Finish up here, and when we're under way and secured, you and your boys help yourselves to a barrel of beer and some drinkin' liquor. I'll tell the steward. Just mind you stay sober enough so we dock at Baton Rouge with the wheel still in the water, y'hear?"

"Yassuh, Cap'n Thorpe, suh! We thank you a lot!"

Jessie shuddered as she saw sailors lifting blistered, scalded pirate bodies and casually dropping them into the sluggish water. She trailed along behind Thorpe and finally asked, "Dumping them like garbage— shouldn't you turn the bodies over to the sheriff? The law?"

Hardly pausing, Thorpe retorted, "Miss Starbuck, this is a documented vessel on a navigable waterway, and I am her master. Which means I am the law, until and unless you officially fire me." Then, before Jessie could respond, he turned to Moran. "Listen, didn't we have a bottle of French stuff when this all started?"

"We did," Moran assured him. "I'll save it from

49

a terrible fate in the saloon, and meet you on the bridge."

Returning with Thorpe to his quarters, Jessie and Ki waited in unspoken agreement until Moran brought the cognac.

"A well-fought battle," Thorpe proposed.

They clicked glasses and drank.

The liquor warmed and relaxed them, and Thorpe showed little emotion when LaFlemme entered to report, "Loading's finished, gangplank's aboard, and steam's up, Captain."

"Fine. What were our losses?"

"Not a soul. Couple of burns from the steam. It must've been hell for them down there," LaFlemme commented. "There is one matter. Nasty business." He glanced toward Jessie, unsure whether he should voice it or not.

"Go ahead," she said wearily. "Nothing you can add could be worse than what I've heard and seen already."

"Yes'm. Sir, there were four men working at the woodlot," LaFlemme related. "Not fifteen minutes before we tied up, they were attacked. Knives, very quiet work. Creoles, maybe some of those renegade Creeks, a couple of whites. One of the woodmen told me just as he was dying. The others are dead too. No sign of the gang who did it. I guess they were scared off by the guards we had along."

"Bastards," Thorpe muttered. "Well, let's get under way."

LaFlemme departed, and Thorpe went out on the promenade. "Pilot, she's all yours," he called out. "Straight on to Baton Rouge, and if any patrol boats hail us, ram 'em!" Then Thorpe came back in and said, "Who's for a nightcap?"

"Cap'n, I may be with drink taken already," Moran declared, breathing heavily. "Best I seek out me bunk."

Ki looked at Jessie, his eyes questioning, then announced, "I'll try the same advice. Good night, all."

After the two men had left, Thorpe canted his head and regarded Jessie. "And as for you, Miss Starbuck?"

"As for me, Captain Thorpe, you may see me to my room."

"It's the least I can do." Taking her arm, he guided her the few steps to her door. But instead of stopping, he continued along with her in tow, her arm still engaged.

"What—?"

"I told you it was the least I could do," Thorpe said. "It's certainly not as much as I *can* do." He steered her for another twenty feet, and through the door of his private stateroom, where for a moment he kept hold of her while he shouted through the pilot-house access hatch. "LeFlemme! I've business here below. You come and go through officer's country, y'hear?"

Overhead, LaFlemme responded with a few words of Cajun patois, and then the hatch slammed shut and latched in place. Releasing Jessie, Thorpe slid the bolt on the promenade door, set up glasses, filled them from a cut-glass decanter, removed his uniform coat and collar and tie, handed his apprehensive guest a glass, and said, "Sit!"

Jessie glanced around. "Where?"

"There're three chairs and a bed. Take your choice."

Jessie opted for the bed. Not because it was suggestive of any budding desires—which were there, she had to admit. For all her antagonism toward Captain Thorpe, she could also sense a perverse little tingling beginning between her thighs, as though her sensuality was responding to his masculine challenge. No, she picked the bed because whatever was going to happen between them would no doubt be preceded by some relentless physical moving about, and she wanted maneuvering room not provided by the seat of a chair.

Thorpe sipped from his glass and stared down at her. She wasn't quite sure whether the hotness of his gaze sprang from anger or lust, but either way she felt confident she could handle it. She'd grown up dealing with prideful, determined men, and the captain could be no worse than those she'd handled in the past.

"Call me Jessie," she said pleasantly, for openers. "I'll call you Gregory, if you don't mind. All right, Gregory, where do we start discussing whatever is on your mind?"

"With what I said earlier. Either I am master of this vessel, or you fire me. It can't be a little bit of both."

"What it *all* is, Gregory, is a Starbuck company."

"If you ever bothered to read the paperwork, you'd know that you may own the company, but that I own eighty percent of the *Dauphine,* just as the other skippers own a share of their boats. If we chose to tie up and go fishing, you'd have a shipping company with no ships. And we'd be stuck with ships and no operating capital, and lots of contracts we'd have to default on. Mexican standoff."

"You're not telling me anything I don't know."

"No?" He began pacing his cabin. "If you knew this business, and the problems we're facing, you would've sent us help—the kind of help we need—instead of coming yourself with no one but your pistolero, or whatever Ki is."

"Ki is an old and valuable friend, no more," Jessie assured him, turning on the bed so the curve of a hip was uppermost. She plucked at her skirt, making sure it draped itself along the sleek lines of her thigh and lower leg. "Have we been that poor? Haven't we been useful at all?"

"Well...I...I 'fess you held your own in that saloon dustup, and you and Ki definitely can shoot. I lost count of how many you yourself put under the water."

"Then you do think I'm good for something, Gregory—I mean, besides the usual role of a woman."

"Who knows if you're any good at *that?*" Thorpe growled, and then glowered at her, as if defying her to be indignant.

Instead, Jessie laughed. "Who knows, Gregory? Who knows if I'm any good as a woman? What gives you reason to presume I'll ever let you find out?"

"Damn you!" Thorpe, goaded by Jessie and his own inner yearnings, spun to the bed. His curling fingers grasped the split fold of her skirt and flipped it up wide, exposing the smooth, flawless columns of her legs to her round, taut-muscled buttocks. He stared unwaveringly at her abbreviated undergarments. "Christ, I don't have to find out, I already know it! The working gals in the staterooms aft of us wear more than you do! You think I can't tell?"

"Gregory, no," she gasped, tugging down her skirt.

"Stop!" But her attempts at modesty were weakening, her resistance ebbing. The man was like a tornado, and who could withstand a tornado? Lord, she wasn't even sure she wished to try.

"I can tell, Jessie—can you?" Thorpe raged, and in an equally stunning move, he released her to grab his shirt in both hands. He ripped it off and slung it aside, looming over her, grinning tauntingly, as if again daring her to rebel, to fire him. "Well, I like to show off my bared chest! What's that tell about me?"

Jessie stared up at him with widening eyes, stared at his broad shoulders, his heavily matted chest, his long, muscular arms, the flat hardness of his belly, and the line of tightly curling hairs that grew down to his belt line. She felt a rising tendril of passion coiling up from her loins, hardening her nipples . . . and then, with a sultry glance lower, she grew achingly aware of the thickening bulge straining against his uniform trousers. Her mouth, lips swelling in anticipation, formed his name.

"Gregory . . ."

"Y'know what it tells?" His hands were at his belt now, loosening the buckle. "It tells you I'm good at bein' a man, so this is your last chance, Jessie!" he warned, panting out the words. "Cover yourself real prim and proper, and walk out that door. Or undress to the buff!"

"Gregory, I—"

"Trouble with you is you talk too damn much!" Again he bent over her, and she trembled in his fingers, which were surprisingly gentle for the steaming urgency she felt emanating from his body. He found the buttons of her jacket and freed them, then parted the thin, expensive silk blouse, exposing the firm, upthrust mounds of her breasts. His big hands closed over the sensitive globes, and she moaned, her heady desires bursting through the last of her restraints.

"Kiss them, Greg . . . kiss them . . ."

His mouth came down, lips wet and hot, mustache rasping her tender flesh. She felt the tip of his tongue dancing from nipple to nipple, and his mouth opening wider, closing on her. She felt a hand fumbling with the catch at her waist and the buttons there, and then realized she was squirming, raising herself to help as he pulled her flared skirt from around her hips. She arched her back, allowing him room to slide down her step-ins and pantaloons, knowing she was baring to him the golden curls of her pubic mound. She panted and mewled, her hands closing on his head, fingers clutching his hair as she felt him pull up.

"Come back . . . come back . . ."

He was out of her arms only long enough to stand, claw the front of his pants open, and shuck them down his legs. He sat on the edge of the bed to kick off his boots and send his trousers after them . . . and then he came back.

Jessie sucked in her breath when she caught sight of the awesome length and girth of his manhood. "You're too big!"

"No, I'm not, Jessie. Not for a woman's who's good," Thorpe retorted, breathing hard, forcing her splayed legs wider. She lay fully open to him, her eyes never leaving the heavily veined erection he would be sinking deep into her yielding flesh... so deep, she sensed, that she would be screaming with exquisite agony.

Then hunching, he knelt between her thighs, his deft fingers brushing through her pubic bush, parting her inner lips and baring her glistening pinkness. He crouched lower...

A shudder rippled through her body as the tip of his eager tongue explored, swirling, lashing her vulnerable loins. She felt his mustache brushing her clitoris, and then his tongue toying, working like an eel deep up inside her, stabbing, twisting, curling...

She cried out, her sleek thighs bucking up to meet his wet loving, clamping tight around his head. He was a master of this too, she thought deliriously.

Her orgasm, when it came, seemed to begin so deep in her belly that she had never known such a spot existed. It was like a million tiny nerve ends all sizzling at once, and she ground her pubic mound involuntarily against his mouth, and heard her own animalistic cries as her release went on and on, as if unending...

And then, with searing suddenness, Thorpe pulled his mouth away. Jessie whimpered in protest, but only for a moment. Then she felt her pulsating loins being invaded, even as she twisted and writhed beneath the assault. She caught her breath as his turgid shaft stretched her entrance incredibly tight, and drilled up into her throbbing sheath.

Her eyes, not focusing well, stared up into his lust-contorted face as Thorpe thrust harder, ramming deeper, hurting her but feeling oh, so good! Without thought on her part, she raised herself up, clamping her legs around his heaving body, helping him sink fully to the hilt.

Their bodies gleaming with sweat, they lay locked together for a minute, catching their breaths. Irrationally she laughed, and murmured, "I tried to tell you, you're too big."

"You lied," Thorpe countered, and began a slow, steady stroking. She found its tempo easy to match, and rotated her hips, feeling her muscles clenching, milking him as he started to piston faster and faster within her. She climaxed again, humping hard against his groin, raking his bucking back with her nails, biting at his chest, panting uncontrollably... and somewhere about that time, she sensed his own completion fast approaching. "Now, Greg, now..."

He slammed in and out of her violently, his mouth gasping out crazed entreaties. And then it was upon him, the explosion, his hot liquid fire rushing to jet far up inside her hungry belly...

The final spending was mutual and total. She lay under him while he kissed her eyes and mouth and ears, licking the salty perspiration away.

"Christ," he muttered, "I could've sworn I'd made you wet enough."

"I was," she sighed. "You weren't."

"Nitpicker." Against her mumured protests, he rolled and his flesh slid out of hers, and he lay beside her. Their naked bodies touched lightly, and his fingers toyed with the damp mass of her hair, and he said, "Maybe next time..."

"Next time? Confident, aren't you, Captain?" She

chuckled throatily as an idea of something flashed through her mind. "All right. But next time, you'll get wet."

Chapter 6

Ki had not gone to bed.

What he'd told the others had been an excuse, pure and simple, in order to politely exit Captain Thorpe's office. And it hadn't been solely for Jessie's sake, either. It had been for his sake as well, to avoid that cognac nightcap. He didn't often drink heavy amounts of liquor, hard or soft, but tonight he'd somehow found himself almost drenched in it.

He'd had enough, and what he really wanted when he'd left was a large mug of steaming hot Louisiana-style coffee. Mud with a lot of chicory stirred into it. However, because of the recent diversions, there was none to be had in the dining room adjoining the saloon. There wasn't even a waiter on hand to fetch any or make some.

So Ki then drifted down to the freight deck, in

hopes that one of the many kids who sold soft drinks and fruit might be in business. He discovered there'd been considerable shifting of, and damage to, the cargo. Sacks that had been watered down or steamed, or both, were sending out a variety of odors, none pleasant. Wagons and carts had been overturned, and at least one pen that had held pigs was now empty, its former occupants running loose, rooting and scrapping with a multitude of cur dogs. Sacks of grain and flour were slopping together in a gooey paste. Tiers of crates and boxes had toppled, smashing open, their contents scattered underfoot. Scores of chickens and ducks were lifeless, feathered lumps in their crates.

This much and more Ki could see by the glow of coal-oil lanterns. What more the rising sun might reveal in a few hours, he didn't feel like guessing. He was sure a lot of shippers would be yelling at the *Dauphine*'s owners, and a lot of insurance carriers also.

Eventually he located a kid who sold him a bottle of something vaguely called "tonic," which he tossed overboard after a couple of swigs. He was turning from the railing when he heard a male voice and a female voice in conflict, then the smack of a palm against flesh, and a feminine yelp of pain, followed by a torrent of curses in Creole or Cajun.

There followed more slapping sounds, interspersed with heavier blows that Ki took to be punches, and cries from the woman. The ruckus seemed to be going on close by, from beyond a mountain of freight to his left. He was not one to intervene in domestic quarrels, but from the sound of it, whoever the woman was, she was getting the pure hell knocked out of her. He made his way over and through the obstacles and saw a man holding on to the arm of a woman as he shook her like a terrier with a rat, punching at her face and squirming body as she kicked and tried to bite. He was a good-sized man with quick, catlike moves, light on his feet, and in this light his complexion was swarthy.

"Slut! You beg me to bring you to New Orleans, and then refuse to take care of the men I send you! And you call yourself a whore!" *Slap! Whop!* "You will learn in a levee crib, and with more than one man at a time!"

"Hey, pimp!" Ki called out. "Enough! I think she's got the idea."

"Who the hell you think you are?" the man barked at him, ceasing his thrashing of his companion to peer into the shadows at the figure of Ki. "Oh, a *nigger!* Geechee nigger, at that. Well, get yo' black ass over here, geechee boy, I'll give you some kicks an' cuts."

Ki hissed. The hiss was a contract, a commitment to personal combat, to the death if necessary, evolved in the Nippon of his maternal ancestors over uncounted generations. The woman was not part of it now, and Ki made no mental note of the fact that, even disheveled, when her face came into the light briefly, it was shown to be delicately boned, with a short, straight nose, soft, full lips that were now bloody, even teeth, and a smooth, symmetrical line of jaw. Her eyes were dark and immense with fear.

Neither was it about the insult the man had launched at Ki. He had long since learned that to give way to anger at a personal slur gave an opponent the very advantage the insult had been intended to achieve.

61

But there was one thing that Ki would not tolerate, a thing that he had learned firsthand as a child in Japan, when he had been rejected by and cast out of his own society. He was a half-blood, the reviled offspring of an American man and a Japanese woman, and it was the irrational hatred of one race for another that he had made it his personal business to confront and destroy wherever and whenever it appeared.

He understood that a "geechee" was a mixture of the blood of blacks with that of Chinese who had been brought to the East Coast to work on such backbreaking projects as railroads and canals, and that such people were held in even lower esteem by the race-haters of the South than were blacks.

It was this stupidity on the part of the man he now faced that he hoped to correct...

Ki presented himself feet-first, leaping into the air after two springing strides, kicking with both heels, aiming for the man's gut. He nearly missed, for his opponent spun smoothly to one side so Ki's right heel barely grazed a hip before he crashed into a bale of something and hit the deck hard but rolling.

Ki realized with surprise that the man was a *savate* fighter, a damned leaping Frenchman, possibly as fast and deadly with his feet as Ki, who was adept in the martial arts of his homeland. Even as Ki came out of the roll, crouched and perfectly balanced, his foe was on the attack, and not merely with his feet.

Light glinted on a long, narrow blade that ended in a needle-thin point, the sort of knife known as an "Arkansas toothpick" farther west. What it was called in Cajun country, Ki neither knew nor cared. His sole interest in the weapon was keeping it from his flesh.

He too had a blade—curving, suggestive of an Arab scimitar, but much shorter than his opponent's weapon, and he carried in addition an arsenal of varied Oriental weapons for throwing and slashing and killing silently at close or far range.

The other man leaped at him, a booted foot slamming into the ridged, iron-hard muscles of Ki's abdomen, bringing a grunt from him, and slamming him backward into a post.

Ki straightened to counterattack, feeling the post rub against his back through his shirt and leather vest, his fingers seeking the handle of the knife in his belt. But Ki barely had time to bob down and to the left, as the long-bladed knife slashed upward, passing a fraction of an inch from Ki's bicep.

As his foe spat out a curse in his patois, Ki made a blade-edge of his callused left hand and slammed it down hard on the other's knife arm, bringing a howl of pain—but not before that slender knife was again flashing toward his throat. Ki sprang back and sent a savage kick to his attacker's midsection, and as the man was bent over by its impact, Ki tried for a killing blow to the base of the skull.

The man escaped death with a movement of no more than a fraction of an inch, and Ki's stiffened fingers buried themselves in muscle rather than bone. It still had effect. The man went sprawling on hands and knees, giving Ki a vital instant, which he used to bring his heel down with bone-smashing force on the other's wrist. The knife went skittering away.

So did the man, scrambling after his knife and trying to regain his feet at the same time. Ki pursued with a series of quick, short kicks, but they lost much of their effectiveness; even the best-aimed blow can do only a limited amount of damage if the person forced to absorb it is moving away.

Yet Ki also realized that the man was not trying to flee. The man had no intention of breaking off the fight, but was looking for a more advantageous place and stance from which to continue it with fists, feet, another knife—experience had taught Ki that a knife fighter usually had a spare handy—or a pistol.

Which was fine with Ki. His overriding intent was to avenge the racism by taking the other's life, but the *savate* fighter was proving difficult to catch, let alone kill. Unless Ki chose to throw one or more of his *shuriken*—and even then, no amount of skill could guarantee an effective strike against such a nimble-dancing target as was eluding him now.

To hell with it, Ki decided in disgust. He had at least partially avenged the prejudice, and could be appeased by prompt and permanent removal of the man from his sight. So he continued his onslaught of kicks, each propelling the man closer to the rail until, vainly attempting to evade Ki, the man tumbled into the murky water with a splash.

Ki ran aft, in case the man succeeded in grabbing something and pulling himself aboard again. But the last Ki saw of him, he was a good fifty yards astern, swimming for shore.

Ki returned to the scene of the fracas, half expecting to find the woman gone. She was still there, however, crouching like a terrified animal between two bales of tanned hides.

"You can come out," he said, offering his hand.

She stayed, quivering. "Is—is he gone?"

"Yes, for a swim. What's your name?"

"A-Annette." She hesitated, then took his hand and rose, allowing him to draw her out. "Annette de Londres."

For the first time, Ki got a proper look at her. She was young and pretty, albeit disheveled. Dark, curly hair framed her cupid face and cascaded below her shoulders. Her blouse was cut low across nubile, unfettered breasts. Her skirt, ruffled with lace, proclaimed her profession by its shortness. And her whole body trembled with fear.

Ki kept smiling. "He's really gone. You're bruised a little, but in a couple of days those will be gone too."

"Only to be replaced by René, when he returns."

The name struck a familiar note. "René? René who?"

"René Duvin, who always returns. And when he does, and when he finds me . . ." The girl shuddered.

René Duvin, the crook-of-all-trades that Moran had mentioned earlier, Ki recalled. Ki saw no need to mention this to Annette, not in her state, and tried to reassure her instead. "I swear, Duvin's a long way astern. There's nothing to worry about now. We'll be in Baton Rouge sometime tomorrow, and you can get off and go home."

"Home? René is my home."

"You must've come from somewhere, Annette."

She crossed her arms as if her shivering were from the cold. "I am Acadian and Indian. My birthplace is—was—New Iberia, to the west. We are all Cajuns there. Jean Lafitte buried his treasure there."

"Really. Well, how far is New Iberia?"

65

"I don't know. Far. Maybe a hundred miles."

"A long way to go just to whore for Duvin."

"I am not a whore. That's the truth."

"I overheard him saying he'd set you up."

"Then you also heard him say that I refused," she retorted, and when that didn't seem to convince Ki, she rushed on bitterly, "René thinks I am one, like you do, because I told him I wanted work of that kind in New Orleans. I told him that because I knew he dealt in women, among other things. It was the only way I could meet him and men like him, men who killed most of my family for no reason."

"Ahhh . . . you hoped to ferret out the killers, whoever they are, through Duvin? How old are you, Annette?"

"Seventeen or eighteen," she said, nibbling her lip.

"Old enough in one respect, but still a child in another. How on earth did you ever convince Duvin you were a prostitute?"

"Stop this!" she cried. "You've helped me and I'm grateful. I'll repay you with the only coin I have, and—and then we will be done with each other, Mister, uh—"

"Ki," he supplied. "I'm not just prying, Annette. A friend of mine owns this boat and others like it. You know the trouble we had tonight. The raiders sound like the same type of scum who wiped out your people. And Duvin is involved in all sorts of dirty business. We might be able to help you, if you'd help by giving us information."

"All right," the girl said, mollified. "I got close to René in the simple way. I lay with him, the *cochon!*" Her eyes were downcast. "He was not the first, but he was the worst. He forced me to pleasure him in disgusting ways. I thought when he finished with me that I could go with any man and not care, because I could not be made lower. But it didn't happen as I believed it would. I had reason to let him use me— I needed him for my revenge—but I could not simply lie down for strange men who paid for me, who paid *him!*"

"So he beat you up."

"He might have killed me if you hadn't stopped him," Annette said. "I owe you my health and my life, maybe."

"Well, someday you might return the favor, maybe," Ki bantered. "Come on, we can't stay here. Come with me."

The girl balked. "Where?"

Ki hesitated, wondering the same. His initial impulse had been to take her to Jessie, Thorpe, and possibly Moran. Yet upon reconsidering, he thought perhaps such haste was unnecessary. Whatever Annette knew, she'd know in the morning, and quite likely she only knew René Duvin as a whoremonger. Even if she did know of some link between Duvin and the raiders, it would do them little immediate good, now that Duvin himself was out of reach.

Moreover, everyone was probably sleeping soundly after their exhausting evening. Moran hadn't been in the saloon, anyway, and Ki couldn't imagine the Irishman being elsewhere other than his bed. And if Jessie and Thorpe were in bed but *not* asleep, Ki would prefer not to disturb them except for an extreme emergency. Besides, Annette was hardly in any condition to be bombarded with questions and answers; she looked precisely what she was, haggard and wan, a battered, crestfallen young girl in sore need of cleaning and resting.

So Ki replied, "To your cabin, Annette."

"No! No!" She dug in her heels.

"Why not? It's paid for, isn't it? And you—"

"I share it with two other girls. René's girls. They'll blame me for this, and mark me worse than René will. Maybe use their razors on me."

"Ah yes, the pimp's loyal stable," Ki murmured sardonically. "Well, the only other place is my quarters."

She shrugged and smiled impishly. "No tricks?"

"No tricks," he replied. "Well, maybe just one— to sneak you up there into the first-class section."

It proved to be no trick at all; Ki and Annette climbed to the Texas deck without meeting a soul. Yet when he ushered her inside and shot the bolt on the door, Annette still gave a slight nervous jump.

"Relax, will you?" Ki told her, lighting the lamps. "Why don't you wash up first, and then I will."

She nodded and, after some trepidation, removed her blouse and skirt, leaving only a thin chemise through which the curves of her lush young figure showed clearly. Her huge eyes were troubled. She went to the washstand, ran water, and carefully soaped her face, wincing often. There were bruises and swellings, but no open wounds—Duvin apparently hadn't wanted to damage his reluctant merchandise to the point where it wouldn't sell—except for an ugly laceration at the corner of her mouth.

Ki daubed a towel into the water, and gently cleaned her wounded lip. "There won't be a scar," he predicted. "Now take off your shoes and climb into bed."

68

She swallowed hard, but did as he suggested. Ki washed the odors of the night from his body, stripping down as if he were alone, then toweled himself dry and slipped into the other side of the bed and bade her good night.

For a minute Annette sat up, clutching the sheet to her breasts. Then she decided. She dropped the sheet and wriggled out of her chemise. Ki, lying on his side facing her, saw purpling bruises over her upper torso, and wished he'd been able to do more damage to Duvin.

Annette reached out for his hand, led it to her breast. Her mouth, wet and open, came down on his, and her tongue explored. She sighed and snuggled closer, sliding a leg slowly up over him.

"No tricks, Annette, that was your idea, remember?" He tried controlling his rising hardness. "Get to sleep."

"But I wish to make love with you," she whispered. "Am I so gruesome from what René did, that you don't want me?" A tear formed in the corner of her eye, and she kissed him more urgently.

Ki broke off the kiss, and tried to hold her at bay as he said, "You're beautiful, lumps and all. But you're—"

"Not good enough?" She wormed close again, and he could feel her warm breath against his cheek, and smell the fragrance of her cleansed skin as she nibbled his ear. "Do you think I am worn out," she whispered, "from too many men?"

"No, just the opposite."

"Then am I a mere babe to you?" Her fingers were moving the coverlet lower, stroking his bare flesh with

69

her fingers as she did so. "Do you think you would be robbing the cradle?"

"You're grown . . . *very* grown," Ki protested. "You're also hurt and upset, and I wonder if you really want what you say."

"Oh, but I do!" Her hands were burning his naked body now, working lower of their own volition, tantalizingly dipping down below the coverlet to circle his belly and loins. She touched him once, lightly, and Ki sucked in his breath, his blood pounding. Then she threw back the coverlet altogether, and her eyes grew smoky and hungry as she gazed down at his rapidly growing erection. She laughed throatily, her pink tongue gliding across her lips. "And look there, Ki, you want the same thing I do."

"You convinced me, Annette. Come here."

She squirmed lengthwise on the bed alongside Ki, and he moved one hand down over the smoothness of her bare buttocks. They were lusciously shaped, and her breasts were warm and soft against his chest. She raised her face and pressed her open mouth tightly against his, and this time he responded fervently, feeling her hand searching down between them. He couldn't help gasping again as her fingers closed around his turgid shaft, and then he crushed the full length of her body against his, grinding his pelvis tightly into her.

"Yes, I want it," she moaned. "I want it now . . ."

Ki pulled her beneath him, and Annette splayed her legs to accept him between them. He could feel her young body throbbing as she slowly undulated her hips against him. Her nubile thighs pressed against his legs as her ankles snaked over and locked around his calves.

Ki plunged deep into her soft, willing flesh while she strained under him. She moaned beneath his thrusts, opening and closing her thighs, her head thrashing from side to side on the bed in total abandon. Ki could feel himself growing and expanding inside her youthfully tight sheath until he felt as if he were going to explode from the exquisite pleasure building in him.

"More! Yes! More!" she pleaded, urging Ki on with the pounding of her heels high on his legs. Then she cried out, piercing the silence of the stateroom. She shuddered convulsively, moaning with delight, as he climaxed violently inside her.

Then her body collapsed limply, and she was still, except for the uncontainable quivering of her thighs pressed firmly around his loins. They both lay quiet, more tired than ever now, and completely satiated.

"Sleep," Ki urged. "There'll be time for us later."

Annette sighed, and the plumpness of her breasts squeezed against his chest. Her hand strayed to his genitals and closed possessively on them, but she did not stroke them. "Yes . . . we'll be very good to ourselves . . . later."

How long they slept, Ki wasn't sure, but bright early sun was slanting through the jalousies when echoing wails and thumpings awakened them. The wild thrashing sounds were filtering in from one of the other staterooms, somewhere along the companionway. Ki suspected that he knew which one.

"Mon Dieu!" Annette bolted straight up. Alarmed, she clutched Ki.

71

He responded. "We might as well forget about sleep now. Just wait it out. In a few hours, there's an important lady I'll introduce you to."

Annette shied away. "Is she nice?"

"Very nice. And right now I think she's being especially nice."

★

Chapter 7

Later, it was with hesitation and misgivings that Annette accompanied Ki to Jessie's stateroom. And it was with captivated relief that she discovered Jessie to be a lovely, charming woman who greeted her warmly. But Annette also found to her surprise that Jessie already seemed aware of her plight, even before being told, for virtually the first thing Jessie said to her was a sympathetic "Oh, you poor dear."

"*Bonjour, madame,*" Annette responded. "Ki saved my life and protected me from a terrible *cochon* of a man."

"Naturally he did," Jessica consoled. "And if a bear had come, he would have saved you from it, too." Looking past the girl, she said, "Ki, what is this?"

Ki introduced Annette, only to be interrupted by a quizzical Captain Thorpe. Ki went on to recount what

73

had happened with René Duvin, and how Annette was involved.

Jessie repeated, "Oh, you poor dear," and this time she meant it earnestly, not merely as a friendly dig at Ki. She led Annette to a chair. "Please, tell us more."

It took a little prompting, but soon the Cajun girl was pouring out her story, releasing with it her pent-up misery, as though she were draining an infected wound.

She related how a marauding gang had destroyed her home village, slaying everyone who could be found. Of her family and close relatives, only her father had survived, and he'd been gravely wounded while insuring her own escape to the bayous. She cried out her grief, and spoke of her confusion over why the attack had occurred, for New Iberia had been isolated, unimportant, its people dirt-poor, dependent for their existence on fishing and hunting. And she confessed to her vendetta, which had impelled her to prostitute herself in the slim hope that she could trace the killers and wreak revenge on them.

Jessie, Ki, and Thorpe listened intently to Annette's every word. As her story of wanton, apparently purposeless murder, torture, and rape unfolded, their faces grew increasingly grim. Like Ki, Jessie and Thorpe quickly perceived the potential similarity between Annette's marauders and the pirates who had been raiding rivercraft—including the *Dauphine* last night. Yet by the time Annette admitted this was her first trip on the Mississippi, all three had realized she was ignorant of any ties between the gangs, or between Duvin and the current rash of plunderings.

When Annette finished, everyone brooded glumly

for a while, until Jessie glanced at the girl and asked, "Did you have a reason to choose Duvin in particular?"

"*Mais oui*. My people fought fiercely against the bandits, and captured one. His tongue was loosened before he was executed. René, he claimed, had supplied their money, whiskey, and guns." Annette gazed down at her feet. "We Cajuns are gentle and kind, unless we are wronged."

Thorpe began, "How was he made to—"

"I don't think we want to know," Ki cut in. "But, Annette, are you sure you learned nothing while you were with Duvin?"

"I learned sporting." She eyed Ki slyly. "René taught, I learned. But he never paraded me to others, he said I wasn't yet ready; and he never talked loosely, not even in his cups. And I was afraid to ask, lest he suspect."

"Dammit, not even a name? Not one lousy name?"

"I'm sorry, Captain Thorpe. The only name René ever mentioned was of the client he was training me for. At first, that is, before I refused to service all the pigs he sent me, and he threatened to sell me to a bordello."

"That's a start," Jessie sighed. "Who was he?"

"I think his name was Pradier—Donetian Pradier."

"I know that Creole bastard!" Thorpe declared. "He heads a New Orleans outfit, the Trois Croix Shipping Company. He ships a lot by us; in fact, he's got cargo aboard now. He'll claim it's destroyed or ruined, and want damages that are outrageous; he always does, at the slightest excuse."

"Besides that, is his company legitimate?"

75

"Far as I hear, Jess—Miss Starbuck. But Pradier himself runs with a wild bunch, mainly the gaming crowd, and seems to prosper whether money is tight or not."

"Worth looking into," Jessie said. "A trading company makes a fine cover for smuggling or fencing operations."

Thorpe nodded. "And the way Pradier floats insurance claims, he could probably fake enough of 'em to get control of one or two steamboat lines that are weak at the bank."

"It might even be worth turning him over to Annette's people," Ki mused, casting a smile at the girl. "I'm sure he'd be willing to talk after some Cajun persuasion."

"I've got a more practical idea," Thorpe said with a snort. "More legal, anyhow. I'll wire Loel Goudron when we dock at Baton Rouge. He's chief of police in New Orleans, with influence in nearly every parish courthouse, and he's well aware of our problems on the river. He's sure to have a fat file on Duvin, so he'll be interested in Annette's tale; and if Donetian Pradier's somehow involved, he'll sniff that out like a Louisiana hound dog chasing a hot coon trail."

The landing at Baton Rouge was made in midafternoon, and the city's waterfront was teeming with activity even in the scorching mugginess of the August day. Wharves were buried under small mountains of freight, and dock laborers bent double under the weight of immense loads. Cranes creaked and shuddered, and the steam engines powering them chuffed and hissed.

Thorpe plunged from the *Dauphine* into the thick

of it, bellowing instructions to his officers and arguing with the dock bosses. Jessie, Ki, and Annette waited for him at dockside, contemplating the thunderheads that were threatening from the south. When he finally broke free to join them, he suggested they make for a tavern uphill, away from the nose-wrinkling smells of the riverside.

"The Red Boar will do for dinner," he predicted. "It's as clean as they come, and serves good food."

A shout halted them before they reached shore, and Moran hurried up, bowling his way through the mass of dockwallopers, pimps, and tarts. He looked well after the diversions of the previous night, and, while greeting her heartily, cast a speculative glance at Annette's bruises. He invited himself along, and the party found carriages to convey them to the restaurant, which was walled in the Spanish style rather than with the open ironwork favored by the French. The aromas of food boiling in pots or sizzling over open fires confirmed Thorpe's recommendation.

A Negro in livery escorted them to a large table, his deferential manner showing that the captain was a frequent and valued customer of the establishment. Pitchers of cold punch were ordered up, with Thorpe advising that nothing from private bottles should be added until the first couple of glasses had had time to make themselves felt. Even the hard-drinking Irishman agreed after a few minutes.

"If I could figure out a way to burn this stuff aboard *Dauphine*, I could forget the damned wood problem," Thorpe maintained, going for his third glass.

Platters of food, laden with a vast variety of sea creatures and meats and vegetables, were borne to them, and eating became a serious business.

"So many delicious flavors in one place," Annette commented at one point.

"Compared to New Orleans, this is a mere *pot-pourri*," Moran replied. "There, they know how to cook!"

"And how long do you think we'll be here, Captain?" Jessie asked with the tone of a proper lady who would never romp with a steamboater. "Don't forget the telegram."

"Written out and in my pocket. How long will we tie up? A day at least. Most of tonight for off-loading cargo, swabbing down after the mess, seeing to some repair and maintenance, and checking boilers and stacks tomorrow morning. We may yet want the loan of *Evangeline*. She's moored next to *Dauphine*, pretty as the day she was christened! And yonder comes Captain Jimmie Fitzhugh himself, looking some the worse for two weeks ashore!"

A man with a build similar to Moran's hove into view. He wore a captain's uniform, but his cap was cocked to one side and far back on his head, and his collar and tie were askew. His full-bearded face showed signs of recent battle. He caught sight of the party and made straight for them.

"And what do we have here?" he bellowed. "'Tis the famous Cap'n Thorpe himself, and at the side of Miss Jessica Starbuck, who should know better, and some innocents dragooned—I mean shanghaied—to pay the bill. I will have a glass with you, Cap'n."

Fitzhugh pulled up a chair, filled a tumbler with punch, and quaffed it rapidly.

Thorpe was clearly holding himself in check, for

he wanted to lay hands on Fitzhugh's boat, and the burly Irishman clearly wasn't sodden enough to let such an event transpire.

With a wink to the others, he went on. "Gregory, ye look in fine fettle, and might I persuade you to come along to the landin', where I want to look into a terrible rumor? I heard some A-rab dhow or Chinee junk or a half-foundered sampan has tied up alongside *Evangeline*. It is me intent to burn same to the waterline." He chuckled.

Thorpe maintained his genial pose and said quietly, "Fitz, *Dauphine* was set upon by a plague of river rats last night. We were lucky. Sent most of them to hell. They were at least sixty strong, which is the biggest raiding party I've heard of yet. Somehow, dynamite was planted in my woodpile, but when it went off, it did little more than kill three of my crew."

The bearded captain looked to the others, then back at Thorpe, and was suddenly very serious. "Well, it's time to talk of mounting cannon."

"Cannon might not help. Not against a swarm of little flat-bottoms. They were all over like flies, along with steam launches," Thorpe countered. "Plenty of well-armed men and a sharp lookout, that's our best bet. Now, I've a problem."

"Another?"

"More of the same. I want to lay over a few days to check out boilers, engines, and stacks. With a full complement of passengers and freight, we all stand to lose a lot of money if there's much delay."

"So?"

"Well, *Evangeline* doesn't go back in service until tomorrow, and you'll be sailing with whatever's left

79

on the dock behind *Dauphine*. So I was thinking perhaps you might charter her to me for the one trip, and
bring *Dauphine* to New Orleans when she's ready.
That way we'd move the most cargo and passengers
and put the most money in our pockets."

"I see what you've in mind," Fitzhugh said. "It
sounds like a reasonable scheme, with good earnings
to be had. If we can be excused here, we can take a
look at *Dauphine*."

"Fine." Thorpe dropped gold coins on the table and
said to the others, "We shouldn't be long."

"Not long a-tall," Fitzhugh agreed.

The two captains departed, chatting amiably.

Jessie sighed. "I was afraid Thorpe would propose
that. I was hoping Fitzhugh wouldn't pick up the
challenge."

"Why not?" Moran declared. "It's him by a knock-
out."

"Thorpe's got height and reach," Ki said.

"A fight?" Annette asked. "Why should they fight?"

Moran countered, "Why do Cajuns fight?"

"For the pleasure of it, among themselves."

"'Tis the same here, colleen," Moran explained.
"And there are matters of principle and business as
well."

Annette turned to Jessie. "Won't you stop it?"

"No. But I won't condone it."

Time passed. Inside of fifteen minutes, pedestrians
could be seen heading for the waterfront at a brisk
pace. Hacks and private carriages and fleet-footed
youths went in the same direction faster than safety
would allow.

"Should we go, Jessie?" Ki asked.

"We'd be crushed by the rabble," Jessie replied, shaking her head, but that was not her real reason for declining.

In a frontier world where men were judged by their brawn, Jessie had witnessed, and enjoyed, her share of fisticuff bouts. And with the possible exception of muleskinners, she knew of no breed more independent and pugnacious than riverboat skippers. But those two rowdies out there were *her* skippers, of *her* company, and she was not about to show any approval of their public brawling.

Another half hour passed before the spectators began to return, and then shortly a hack appeared. In its rear, disheveled, bloodied, their clothes filthy and ripped to shreds, rode the two captains, tipped together. The hack halted and, gallantly attempting to assist each other out, both men fell into the street, groaning.

"All bets are off," Moran ruled. "It's a draw."

"Whiskey," Fitzhugh muttered, feeling a tooth.

"And icepacks," Thorpe added, wincing.

Jessie asked tersely, "Was an agreement struck?"

"Compromise," Thorpe replied. "We use *Evangeline,* with Captain Fitz in command, but with *Dauphine*'s crew."

"Is that wise?"

"It's the best we can do, ma'am," Fitzhugh told her. "My crew's been ashore a long while, and is less in shape."

"Then it's settled," she snapped. "How it was settled will be gone into at a later date. Captain Thorpe, I assume you'll see to the details of the transfer."

"Consider it done, Miss Starbuck."

81

"And we'll need suitable lodging."

"The Chateau d'Lambert. It's so fine, even the hack drivers can't take you there without directions."

"Then I leave it in your hands," Jessie retorted. "It's been a long time since I toured the old city of Baton Rouge. I'm sure Annette would enjoy a ride. If you would hail a phaeton . . . and Ki, keep an eye on these louts, will you?"

When, later, she was ensconced in the Chateau d'Lambert, Jessie felt pleased that she'd accepted Captain Thorpe's recommendation. She was utterly enchanted by its high ceilings and ornate moldings, crystal chandeliers, gleaming napery and china, and lantern-lit formal garden with its flowering shrubs and moss-bearded oaks. She found the formally dressed guests delightful, and the hotel's concierge a marvel fluent in five languages.

She demonstrated her pleasure to Captain Thorpe in inventive and exhausting, though thoroughly satisfying fashion.

Chapter 8

All factors considered, the substitution of *Evangeline* for *Dauphine* went off with few hitches. There was some grumbling from passengers at the inconvenience of shifting to the other craft, but the battle with the raiders had left the *Dauphine* cosmetically rough and uncomfortable.

Ki stayed close to Annette, because she wanted him to. She feared that Duvin might have a confederate still aboard, one whom he might have ordered to eliminate her before he'd been dumped into the river. Ki questioned the girl's logic, but didn't argue, enjoying the arrangement anyway.

Jessie, on the other hand, contrived to keep her distance from Captain Thorpe, in order for him to concentrate on the transfer without interference. Hers was not a difficult feat, because he was tied up most of the time, holding his ground in the delicate balance of power that existed between himself and Fitzhugh.

The crewmen presented another difficulty. Although Fitzhugh was nominally in charge, and had his own first and second officers along, the vast majority of men working the vessel were Thorpe's. In a conflict on the bridge, they would instinctively side with him. Both captains knew it was vital to avoid such a confrontation. The trip would be brief, but could leave deep scars if handled wrongly.

Minutes before they cast off, a telegram was delivered to Thorpe. It had been sent from New Orleans by Chief of Police Goudron, and stated: *Watching Pradier, hunting Duvin. Present all interested parties immediately upon arrival, Hotel de Ville days, Hotel Negresco nights.*

When Thorpe showed the message to Jessie, she commented, "Hotel de Ville's the city hall, I know, where Goudron must have his office. Does he live at the Negresco?"

"I assume so," Thorpe said with a shrug.

"The Negresco's in the same class as the Chateau d'Lambert. How could a police chief afford it?"

"Goudron's independently wealthy. Scion of a great family, and all that." Thorpe repocketed the telegram, and as he turned to resume his shipboard tasks, he sighed dramatically. "That was my first major mistake in life; I failed to pick rich parents."

During departure, Jessie retired from the turmoil to her stateroom. She took from a well-concealed pocket in her trunk a small, leatherbound black book, then settled in a chair by the open jalousies and began thumbing through the book, pausing occasionally to

84

study one or another of its pages.

The book was a smaller facsimile of an original volume that Jessie kept in her father's old desk back at the Circle Star Ranch in Texas. In fact, much of the original book was in her father's handwriting; he had begun compiling the information it contained when Jessie was a small child. The remainder was in Jessie's hand; after her father's death, she had continued adding to and revising Alex Starbuck's already exhaustive entries. The book was a priceless collection of data, listings and cross-listings of every person and organization known to be even remotely connected with the shadowy international conspiracy that Jessie and Ki knew simply as "the cartel."

The copy she was presently perusing was her traveling version of the original, abbreviated and written in a personal code that only Jessie understood. She easily found a listing for the Trois Croix Shipping Company, though there was no mention of anyone named Donetian Pradier. Decoded, the entry read:

Trois Croix is a likely conduit of provisions and arms to a loose group of renegades involved in terror acts in the Deep South. Possible recruiting function; makeup of bands may be deserters or malcontents from both sides of the Civil War, runaway slaves, Creek and Cherokee and perhaps Seminole Indians. Motive unknown, but may be simple race hatred, of northern Europeans and English in particular; Louisiana Purchase displaced many French, Spanish, and Indians from farms, tribal lands, etc. Thus far, Trois Croix's actions seem to be focused on harassment of whites moving west. Trois Croix may be one of many similar organizations used by the cartel to further its own ends. See cross-references.

Jessie looked further through the book, scanning the names of individuals and companies somehow linked to Trois Croix. She was aware that much of the information might be out of date, since it had been set down by her father while she was still a child. Yet the name of one New Orleans firm brought to mind something Colin Moran had mentioned at their initial meeting after the free-for-all. Intrigued, she returned the book to its trunk compartment, and went out looking for the Irishman.

It was a short hunt. She headed straight for *Evangeline*'s saloon and found him there, comparing its stock of spirits with *Dauphine*'s.

"G'mawning, Miss Starbuck. What can I do for ye?"

"What firm did you say Sykes works for?"

"Ah, that one! And well rid of his carcass we are. His employer is Continental Express, in New Orleans. A factoring firm, shipping and receiving, and shady to boot."

"To and from where? Which ports?"

"European, mostly, with a wee dabblin' in Mexico and South America. Why?"

"I suspect Continental Express does, or did, business with Trois Croix. Could you, well, look into this?"

"My pleasure."

"You might hear things about Pradier and Duvin, too."

"No doubt more'n you'd care to know. The difficulty is always siftin' out the few kernels of fact from the mass of fancy," Moran observed. "But I'll be able to get help from those I'm normally after attemptin' to outwit."

"Come now! Your enemies won't help you."

"In a matter such as this, they will. Any group that is a global power is a threat to all countries. We'll become uneasy bedfellows as long as necessary, and then back to doin' each other dirty as usual."

"I'll take your word for it," Jessie said dubiously. "In any case, let's keep this between ourselves. Captain Thorpe is rather, ah, blunt in his approach, and against the cartel, that could get him killed."

"We wouldn't want that on our consciences, would we?" Moran winked, and waved to the barman for a refill.

The voyage proved to be a fast one, there being no landings en route. Fitzhugh ordered a few extraneous and complex maneuvers to be performed—this was, in reality, a shakedown cruise after a major refitting— but despite these and the normal complicating frazzles, the running time came in under twenty-six hours.

It was late evening when the *Evangeline* finally snugged tight, and gangplanks were lowered to the Toulouse Street wharf. If Baton Rouge had appeared busy by day, New Orleans was downright bedlam by night, and Thorpe was more than happy to turn the problems of cargo and passengers over to Captain Fitzhugh. After all, as he told Jessie, he was certainly an "interested party," and Chief Goudron's telegraphed request was virtually a summons he couldn't ignore.

Accompanying Jessie and Thorpe were Ki, Annette, and the indefatigable Moran. They walked up to Moon Walk Quai, where they hired a coach to take them to the Hotel Negresco, in the heart of the glamorous French Quarter.

The Negresco was a graceful three-story structure, partially concealed behind delicate balconies, great oaks, and gum trees. Gaslights illuminated its façade, and other carriages were delivering expensively dressed parties when the five pulled into the courtyard. Alighting from the coach, they went through huge, ornate doors into a plush-carpeted lobby, and approached the registration desk.

They were greeted by the manager himself, who recognized Jessie from prior visits. "My, Miss Starbuck, so good to see you back. Will y'all be staying over?"

"Yes," she replied, in snap decision, and glanced at the others. Moran shook his head, indicating that he was to be excluded, and Thorpe would be bedding aboard the ship, at least ostensibly. "Three rooms, preferably connecting, and please have our luggage brought from the *Evangeline*."

"At once. Rooms 207, 209, and 211 should do."

The manager dispatched a bellhop to the wharf while Jessie, Ki, and Annette signed the register. Annette was shy about it, as though she didn't belong in such a high-tone place—and indeed she wouldn't have, if she'd still been wearing her bawdy-cut blouse and skirt. Instead, the girl was attired in a fashionable two-piece, powder-blue suit, bought for her by Jessie in Baton Rouge.

Then Jessie said, "I believe Chief Goudron is expecting us to call. Could you direct us to his room?"

"He's in Suite 124, Miss Starbuck, end of the hall."

"Thank you."

The man who answered their knock on Suite 124's door was an impeccably dressed skeleton with curly dark hair and luxuriant sideburns framing his thin Gallic face.

"Loel Goudron, at your service," he said as introductions were passed. And when he bowed low over Jessie's hand, his policeman's eyes expertly appraised the swell of her breasts, while he murmured: *"Enchanté, mam'selle."*

Jessie flashed her obligatory dazzling smile, and made a mental note to keep close check on the buttons of her clothing. But Goudron became all business after that—politely so, but official nonetheless—seating them comfortably in his elegant bachelor's flat, and giving his total concentration to absorbing their various accounts.

"The most ambitious piracy yet," he said at last. "If your estimate is correct, it's grown beyond being a small group of cutthroats, and become a major operation."

"Fifty raiders at a minimum," Thorpe insisted. "And who knows how many more ashore and in boats out of range."

"Plus others planted aboard, set to help when the time was right." Ki rubbed an earlobe thoughtfully. "I bet they're the cause of that apparently senseless fight on the cargo deck. It was intended as a diversion."

Moran nodded agreement. "Might well've worked, too, if it hadn't been merely by chance that 'twas the very same moment I was startin' my punch-up with Tom Sykes. That would've disrupted their schedule, I'm after thinking."

"A fortunate happenstance. But if they had succeeded, what would they have gained?" Goudron asked. "What were they after, to launch such a large and organized attempt?"

"There were jewels and money, but nothing fabulously valuable aboard that I know of," Thorpe answered. "They weren't planning to steal *Dauphine*, not if they put dynamite in the fuel bunker. They couldn't run it in the bayous, anyway."

Jessie, who'd been quietly contemplating, suddenly spoke up. "It was cargo. Nothing else would require all those men, or those flatboats they were towing." She turned to Thorpe. "Was Pradier shipping lots of freight this trip?"

"Yes, and heavy too. I'd have to check the manifests to learn the contents, though there's no guarantee that what's claimed is true. My rec'lection is we took it all on at Natchez, which is as far north as we go."

"Me'n Duvin boarded at Natchez!" Annette declared.

"I just heard another link drop in place," Ki said. "Duvin was along to oversee the cargo, and maybe the raid too."

"I'm wonderin' if it wasn't Sykes instead." Moran hunched forward, waggling a finger at Chief Goudron. "Now that sod is in hospital at Baton Rouge, if he hasn't the manners to die. Your counterpart there might squeeze some information from Sykes, if ye were to suggest a questioning."

Goudron just sat there for a moment, looking sourly at Moran. Then, excusing himself, he went to an inner door of the suite. A uniformed officer, evidently of high rank, appeared, and the two conferred awhile in low, subdued voices.

When Goudron dismissed the officer and returned to his seat, he said, "Very well, I'm sending a wire to Baton Rouge. I'm also having all freight consigned to Trois Croix impounded for inspection, and the same for any destined for Continental Express." His expression darkened to a half-scowl. "And I am informed that René Duvin has reportedly been spotted here in New Orleans. A thorough search is being instigated of places he's known to frequent."

"The *cochon!*" Annette swore. "If I find René first, he will be delivered to you with a knife between his ribs."

"Don't even try," Goudron warned. "Leave it to us."

"But I could find him, and faster than all your police," the girl insisted defiantly. "I could, because René will want to find me. To silence me before I can tell on him."

"You don't know anything to tell," Jessie reminded her.

"Can René be sure of that? Can he remember every word he spoke to me? No! If he hears I am out looking for him, he will come after me, believing me to be a danger."

"You're definitely that," Ki quipped. "But before you could get at him or get help, he'd get you. Murder you."

"A risk I accept, always have. I only live, and will

91

die, for my revenge." She eyed Ki intently, a slight quirk to her lips. "And you'd protect me, *non?* If René heard you were with me, he'd have double reason to show himself."

Struck by the force of Annette's determination, Ki turned to Jessie, who looked equally amazed. And yet, in exchanging glances came the remembrance of their own driving need to uncover and destroy the cartel. With it came understanding: they could not deny Annette her cause.

"You'd be bait in a trap, Ki," Jessie warned.

"Yes, but it might be worth a try."

"Aye, the colleen does make a point," Moran allowed. "Here's hopin' she never takes such a dislike to meself."

"You wouldn't be bait in a trap," Thorpe protested. "You'd be meat thrown into a wolves' den! Chief Goudron, certainly you're not going to allow this suicidal scheme!"

"I cannot permit it."

"You cannot stop it," Annette argued crossly. "You cannot stop me, unless you lock me in your prison forever."

"*Sacre,* such venom from a *jeune fille.*" Goudron sighed the sigh of a man plagued by women. "Rather than detain you, *Mam'selle* de Londres, I shall assign an officer to accompany you wherever you roam. He will look and dress the part of a dock thug. Do you agree to comply with this?"

After hesitating at first, Annette finally nodded.

"Good. I hold you to your bond," Goudron said, and shifted to regard Thorpe. "Captain, I need you to volunteer."

"Name it."

"I'd like you to go to the wharf and be available to my men, should they want help in identifying Pradier's cargo."

"I was thinking to do that anyway. If I don't check the freight, he's liable to hit us with a massive claim for damages to his merchandise, and win by default."

"And while you're having a run at the dark side of New Orleans night life," Moran said, "I'll be looking after me own bit o' business."

"And just what am I supposed to be doing while all this is going on?" Jessie demanded. "Sitting in my room?"

Thorpe made the mistake of saying, "Sounds reasonable to me. It's rough along the waterfront, and you're dressed—"

"Not if my trunks have arrived," she cut in tersely. "If you'll all excuse me a minute?"

She strode from the room without another word.

Thorpe sank his head into his hands, and muttered about ornery females going where angels fear to tread. "The alleys of the French Quarter run with blood every night, and the closer to the river, the more the blood."

Moran chuckled. "Bucko, if you plan on leavin' her behind, ye'd best be chaining her to something solid."

"I suspect she'd break any chain I have," Goudron said. "But she should be safe enough with us and my men nearby."

Almost ten minutes passed before Jessie reappeared, and it was obvious her trunks had indeed arrived. In place of her smart traveling ensemble, she was changed into a snug-fitting beige chambray shirt,

93

tight, well-worn jeans, a denim jacket, a wide brown leather belt, and riding boots. Her custom-made Colt .38 pistol rode holstered on her right thigh; and unknown to all except Ki, a twin-shot derringer was secreted behind the large plate buckle of her belt.

She smiled pleasantly at them. "I'm ready now."

Chapter 9

Squads of police were already at the Toulouse Street wharf when their chief, Jessie, and Thorpe arrived.

So was Donetian Pradier, outraged that his freight had been quarantined. A towering, swarthy man in a frock coat and a planter's hat, Pradier greeted the trio with a voluble torrent of French and English, the gist of which was that he was the victim of thieves and the target of chicanery, whose purpose was obscure to him.

"Shut up," Goudron ordered him quietly, and sank the metal knob of his walking stick into the big man's belly. "A lady is present. Your language is offensive."

Pradier, doubling over and grunting with pain, glared ominously. "And impounding my goods is illegal," he panted.

"Not when infestations of boll weevil larvae are

suspected; but by all means, take your complaint to a magistrate. For now, m'sieu, present your documents."

Eyes narrow, face flushed with rage, Pradier withdrew an oilskin packet from inside his coat, and handed it over.

Goudron moved over to take advantage of a gaslight as he slit the seal and unfolded the contents. He said conversationally, "Just hardware and woollen goods, hm? Perhaps I was wrong..." Then he turned and called to the police guarding the cargo, "Break open those crates! *Vite!*"

"Goudron, I swear you'll regret this before sunrise!" Pradier raved. "I am a respected businessman, and—"

"You are a businessman, but I am chief of police. It is my duty to make sure there are no larvae, that the manifest is not false. All too often, merchants such as yourself are victimized by rogues who sell one thing at a distance and ship another, only to steal it from the docks before it reaches your warehouse. Does this not happen?"

Suspiciously, Pradier muttered a sullen assent.

With a screech of nails, the lid of the first crate was finally pried off. A layer of blankets was removed to reveal racks of Winchester repeaters, two dozen in all, gleaming with protective oil.

"Are these what you ordered as 'hardware,' m'sieu?"

"Of course not," Pradier snapped. "Obviously the shipper made some mistake. He's the one at fault, not me."

As the process continued, the wharf became strewn

96

with an assortment of carbines and revolvers with appropriate ammunition, as well as machetes, small bombs, dynamite and caps and coils of fuse, and other impedimenta of warfare. Jessie and Thorpe watched astounded while crate after crate disgorged more smuggled weaponry, until Goudron, in a tone of ill-concealed disgust, announced it was time to move on.

"To my offices, and, m'sieu, you will come with me," Goudron told Pradier. "I expect your coopera-tion. No doubt you're even more eager than I to de-termine how such a consignment could have been misdirected to your hands."

"But I must begin my own inquiries," Pradier blus-tered. "I must speak with my managers, and cable my shippers."

"And I have handcuffs," Goudron responded. "Whether you wear them or not is entirely up to you."

Pradier glowered but made no further protest, as two burly uniformed officers moved up to flank him. They all left the wharf then, and trooped to the quay-side, where an enclosed police wagon was waiting. Pradier was bundled into the van with his escort, and after a word with the driver, Goudron waved him to go. He strolled over to where Jessie and Thorpe, somewhat puzzled, were waiting.

"It will take them a long time to reach my offices— sufficient time that a warrant to search Pradier's ware-house and office can be obtained. I doubt, though, that much will be found."

"There's enough stuff on the wharf to provision a revolution, so there must be a lot more at his ware-house."

"Probably some firearms and knives, Miss Starbuck, but they'll be legitimate. Pradier's a licensed weapons dealer, and he's too shrewd to store his contraband where it can be readily discovered. My guess is that the crates would've been transported within hours to a hidden cache."

"So what will we turn up?" Thorpe pressed.

"Harmless provisions—flour, bacon, coffee, soft goods, medicinals—scheduled for shipment in the next few days. Also the names and locations of firms selling Pradier his legal firearms, especially those up North."

"That makes sense," Jessie said. "We know the contraband tonight came from the North, even if the manifests are false. With luck, a little cross-checking might turn up which of his suppliers are also crooked."

Goudron shook his head. "What bothers me is that if the raid had worked as planned, Pradier would've had his contraband and stuck our insurance carriers for the loss. The man is plumb inventive."

"We must see to making that the past tense, Captain Thorpe," Jessie vowed, "to making Pradier ancient history."

Goudron's prediction turned out to be correct.

After several hours of combing Pradier's warehouse, they found nothing questionable, much less incriminating, and Goudron called a halt to what was becoming a waste of time.

"But I'm not through with Pradier," he promised. "I'll bury him in paper till he won't be able to ship a sack of salt for a week. That should hurt his schedule."

"There's something else you and your men could do," Jessie suggested. "If you checked through his invoices for previous shipments, you might find a pattern to them."

Thorpe asked, "What kind of pattern?"

"A direction, maybe, where large orders of provisions—enough to feed a small army—were sent on a regular basis. I'd guess west, into the bayous."

"Excellent idea, Miss Starbuck, I'll put someone on it right now." Goudron walked away to locate that someone.

Thorpe said to Jessie, "I don't know if that'll solve the problem of pinpointing the raiders' hideout. There're hundreds of square miles of bayou, and boats don't leave tracks."

"Well, what else can we do, Greg?"

"Nothing, for the moment. Except go get some well-earned sleep, or better yet"—he grinned foxily—"go to bed."

★

Chapter 10

"What a sewer," Ki remarked, as they left yet another smoky, noisy riverfront dive. "To water the rotgut would be an act of mercy."

The man with him chuckled. His name was Boucher, and he was the officer assigned to Annette— but he was also, as promised, a plug-ugly dockwalloper, barrel-chested and mean-faced, wearing a soiled striped shirt, grubby corduroys, and mucker's boots.

"Too bad we can't be hunting a man of higher class," Boucher responded. "But this's the level where Duvin will be found, *if* he is to be found."

"He will be, when he comes to find us," Annette said. Sandwiched between Boucher and Ki, the Cajun girl was fittingly dressed in her skimpy blouse and skirt again, and had lost none of her earlier fervency.

Yet, despite her bravado, Ki sensed that she was

becoming increasingly nervous as they prowled the French Quarter and Jackson Square byways. Each time they pursued a report of Duvin being here or there, and arrived to learn he'd already moved on, Annette seemed to quiver just a little bit more, her fingers trembling against the sharp, stilettolike knife she'd hidden beneath her blouse.

Ki wasn't surprised. To Annette, New Orleans would be an unfamiliar threat. She was accustomed to such dangers as snakes, alligators, and wildcats, having grown up in the bayous; but she was still very much a stranger to the savageries of big-city swamps.

They walked down to the intersection of Canal and Royal, where on one corner was a scabrous deadfall with a sign proclaiming it to be the Ship's Cat. Appropriately, it was across the street from another, called the River Rat.

The louvered barroom door flapped shut behind them, and they entered a room about thirty by fifty feet. The Ship's Cat had a floor strewn with sawdust and peanut shells, soggy with an ancient blending of sweat, urine, rodent droppings, and the spillage from cheap, raw liquor. Its wet reek didn't appear to bother the boisterous sailors, laborers, harlots, and knaves who jammed the bar and surrounding tables.

Nor did the customers act particularly concerned with any temporary lapse of service caused by the bartender standing motionless in abject fear. No wonder; the point of a long, thin skinning knife was being held against the man's Adam's apple. The knife's holder was René Duvin.

"Duvin!" Boucher shouted, reaching for his pistol.

Duvin whirled, thrusting the bartender away as he

101

angled to make his escape through the rear of the tavern. The hammer of Boucher's pocket pistol snagged in his pants pocket, delaying his draw. But Ki was already in motion.

Knocking Annette aside to keep her out of harm's way, Ki sprang straight at Duvin, simultaneously plucking a *shuriken* from inside his vest. He saw Duvin shove into the startled crowd and become slowed by its muddy confusion, and he knew he would reach Duvin before the man could reach the rear door. Duvin, evidently realizing the same thing, pivoted about on the ball of one foot, to face Ki with his skinning knife in one hand and a sleeve derringer in his other.

The knife was no throwing weapon, but the stubby hideout gun could be accurate enough within a ten-yard range. Even if Duvin missed, just the thunder of a shot and the resultant chaos might buy him enough time to get to the door.

"You slant-eyed shit!" Duvin snarled, squeezing on the trigger. "This time—"

The first of Ki's *shuriken* whirred through the air and sawed into its mark, slicing through the fleshy web between thumb and forefinger, severing the tendons of Duvin's gun hand. His thumb flopped uselessly, and his derringer dropped to the floor. The derringer was still falling when Ki's second *shuriken* neatly separated Duvin's nose and upper lip from his face, leaving a gout of spurting blood in its wake.

With a bubbling howl of agony, Duvin staggered backwards and lurched blindly toward the door. The crowd no longer stood in his way, having parted from around him in a stampede for cover. Duvin stumbled, blundering against the counter. Ki was almost upon him. Then the bartender, having grabbed a sawed-off shotgun, tripped both its barrels at point-blank range, and blew Duvin's head apart.

Shredded flesh and bone sprayed the room, and what a second before had been a living human being smacked wetly against the opposite wall. It shriveled to the floor, adding its crimson juices to the sodden covering of sawdust and shells.

The barroom was reverberating from the twin shotgun blasts, and powdersmoke was drifting out through the louvered entrance. Boucher, standing with his back to the door, had his pistol trained stiffly with both hands, but the customers were making no move to leave. They were all too stunned to do more than cower, at least for the moment. Annette was slumped against the bar, her face pale and averted, as she fought the urge to be violently ill.

And Ki, infuriated, wrenched the shotgun out of the bartender's shaking grasp. "I wanted to stop him," he snapped, "not kill him!"

"H-he was gonna kill me," the bartender pleaded. "You musta seen that when you come in."

"Why was he?"

The bartender groaned, and placed both hands on the wood for support. Sweat was streaming down his face.

Hefting the shotgun by its barrels, Ki swung it hard against the counter, cracking its stock. *"Why was he?"*

The bartender blurted, "Jesus, mister! Take it easy! R-René, he was asking about a girl."

"A particular girl?"

"Y-yeah. Some kinda young Cajun whore, it was, who would've been in asking for him. Can't rec'lect the name, but his description kinda fits the gal you came in with, no offense intended. Hell, I ain't seen her, ain't even heard of her, but René, he was desp'rate. He wanted her bad."

"That's all?"

"That's enough, when René don't believe a feller."

By now the boozy customers were over their initial shock, and were wailing and shouting, on the verge of fleeing, especially those with something to hide. Ki wasn't sure whether Boucher could hold them— or, for that matter, why he should try—and judging by the expression on Boucher's grizzled face, he was wondering much the same.

Ki moved from the counter to help, just as the frantic customers broke. And just then, uniformed policemen poured in from the street, while a second wedge crashed through the rear door. The customers bolted, scattering and resisting.

The ensuing melee was bitter and loud, but short-lived. The converging police were met with bottles and fists, but quickly restored order by bunching the customers together and laying waste with swinging nightsticks and pistols.

Before it was over, Boucher and Ki and Annette were conveniently allowed to slip through the police cordon. While the police turned a blind eye, they scuttled along the backbar, stepping over the bartender, who was sprawled on the planking, having been smacked comatose by a nightstick to the ear. Then, diving through the rear doorway, they ran through a tiny storeroom and toward the tavern's back exit, which opened out into a muddy alley.

Flinging open the rear exit's door, they were just

starting to step into the alley when the bomb exploded.

The blast lit the dark alley with a burst of orange fire. Its violent concussion knocked them flat, and sent a number of policemen and curious bystanders crashing into walls or to the pavement. Doors were caved in, windows shattered, and where the alley met the street, the corner of the saloon collapsed into rubble.

Severe as the havoc was, much greater destruction and death would have resulted if the bomber had not made a slight miscalculation: he'd either cut the fuse about two seconds short, or had been that much too slow with his toss. So the bomb—estimated later to have been three or four dynamite sticks taped together—erupted midway through his throw, some thirty feet away from the back exit's door, and almost that high above the cobblestones.

Ki, from the corner of his eye, had glimpsed the sparks of the fuse on the hurtling bomb and, down by the street, a figure turning to run away. Yet even his swift, trained reflexes could do little to save them. He bowled against Annette when the bomb detonated, and went down with her in a tangled heap of arms and legs, while Boucher pitched backwards into the saloon's storeroom.

Fetching up against the alley wall of the building, Ki struggled to his knees, gasping for breath and looking about with unfocused eyes. As he blinked, he caught another fleeting impression of the running figure; it was hardly more than a blur to Ki, but a large blur, retreating along the continuation of the alley across the street.

He scrambled upright and set out in pursuit. Between him and the street was an obstacle course of bodies, some of whom lay motionless in grotesque poses. More devastation littered the street, along with survivors writhing and screaming. But the way was clear when he reached the other side, and he plunged headlong into the next section of alley as fast as he could run.

Somewhere behind him a burst gas line was shooting out a long tongue of blue-orange flame, eerily lighting the scene of carnage. It helped Ki to see ahead, where the dark silhouette of his quarry was madly dashing, trying to widen the distance between them.

Ki sprinted after the figure, trying to close the gap. And as he hit his full stride, he began unwinding his *surushin*, his rope belt with its weighted ends, from around his waist. He held the lead weights in one hand while he straightened the braided rope with the other, preparing to bring his arcane weapon into play at the first opportunity.

For that, however, he had to get nearer. Then, if his aim was true, the bomber would go no farther. Ki well knew the effectiveness of his *surushin*, having practiced with it at the Circle Star Ranch, dropping thousand-pound steers while galloping on horseback. Yet Ki was also aware that if one of the weights should strike a vital spot, it would kill with the force of a bullet.

A dead man would do him no good.

Ki pushed himself faster, determined to overtake his quarry before he could reach the alley's far end, and perhaps lose his pursuer in the crowded streets beyond. Gradually he was gaining, Ki realized, for now he could perceive a sharper image—that of a man, a big man the way Captain Thorpe was big, moving with great speed and agility for his size, but running a bit unevenly, as if weighted down. The man was wearing some type of close-fitting hat or cap that made a black lump of his head, and he did not look back.

Chance intervened. The man tripped on some obstruction and almost fell to his knees. He recovered quickly, but his stride had been broken sufficiently for Ki to close to within fifty feet.

Ki started whirling his *surushin*. Faster and faster it circled, until it was a whining, near invisible creature in the air around him. Then he let fly.

Spinning end for end, the *surushin* hurtled toward the man, its weights building up a tremendous arcing force. Leaping along behind, Ki could see it going too low for the head; it would hit somewhere below the man's chest.

The man glanced back for an instant. As he turned, swiveling to alter his direction, the *surushin* struck him and coiled inexorably about his body, pinning his right arm to his side, one weight hitting above the left kidney, the other in the area of his groin. With a sharp cry of pain, the man collapsed.

Ki had his *tanto* drawn by the time he caught up with his victim, who already was almost to his feet, trying to cast off the binding rope. The tumble had knocked off his hat, and Ki stiffened in shock at the sight of frosty white hair cut very short, close to the massive skull. The man's features were contorted in rage, and a guttural curse spewed from the snarling mouth.

107

The curse was in German: *"Scheisse!"*

"Von Eismann!" Ki gasped. "You can't be!"

"Mein Gott, der Japaner," the Iceman grunted in similar amazement. He'd one foot under him already, and most of his weight was on his left knee, as he struggled to free himself and attack. "So, once more we meet, eh?"

Ki responded with a hasty snap-kick, his shock overcome by his hatred and by his instinct to stop Von Eismann before he tore loose. Von Eismann ducked, and the kick grazed off his right cheek, shoving him off balance. Ki saw his chance—maybe his only chance—and drew his *tanto* as he leaped again.

Frantically, Von Eismann wrenched around and blocked Ki's strike with his unbound left forearm. The blade punctured his sleeve and scraped against metal, as Von Eismann countered by swiveling his wrist, trying to lock Ki's knife in his mechanical hand.

Ki jerked away an instant before the ratcheting steel fingers could clamp shut, his blade's edge slicing the palm of the hand's black glove and glancing off the thin, metallic nails that protruded from the fingertips. Then, pivoting, Ki loosed another kick, this one finding its mark in Von Eismann's solar plexus. It had the power to make kindling out of a normal man's ribcage, but seemed to accomplish little more than knock some wind and a growl of pain from the Prussian.

He must be wearing armor under there, Ki thought, as the jolt of his contact streaked painfully through bone and muscle, up his leg to his pelvis.

And Von Eismann allowed him no respite, lunging at Ki while breaking free from the last of the *surush-*

in's coils. Ki dipped back not an instant too soon, as five talonlike fingernails raked his loose-fitting shirt, shredding its front and leaving angry red lines that oozed blood. An inch closer, and that articulating hand would have hooked beneath his lowest rib, ripping into his lungs and piercing his organs.

"Verdammt! When will I ever kill you?"

I could ask you the same, Ki thought bitterly, dropping into a crouch. The last time they'd met, he'd seen the Iceman go over a cliff four hundred feet above the Gila River in Arizona, and had heard the man hit the water with a force no human could survive. Yet here he was once more, and Ki would have to kill him—again.

Or be killed—for Von Eismann was rearing up, and Ki sensed the closeness of death in his heavy Teutonic features. His bushy, frost-white eyebrows quivered as Ki launched a fast *teisho* strike, which, if it had found his nose, would have shattered the cartilage and driven it in shards through his brain.

But the Iceman reacted with equal swiftness, canting his head enough so that the strike skewed harmlessly off his massive jaw. This brought Ki in sufficiently close to become trapped by the looping arc of the artificial hand.

Ki squatted while simultaneously backpedaling, aware from cruel experience how that encircling arm could crush him. He could not entirely avoid the grasping fingers, and this time they snared enough of his knife to wrench it from his grip. It flew away as Ki rained a series of stiff-handed blows, and Von Eismann countered with blocks and jabs.

Their close proximity put Ki at a disadvantage,

now that he had lost his knife. He still had *shuriken,* but not the distance he needed to spin them. And to bring into play his more powerful kicks, he also needed more space than Von Eismann was allowing him. At this range, Von Eismann could slug it out, letting his proficiency in martial arts and that armor he was wearing absorb Ki's chops and elbow slams, while continually boring in to prevent Ki from gaining any space between them.

Abruptly, from the mouth of the alley behind them, came a sundering roar and a sky-filling orange light. The ruptured gas pipe had set the tavern and adjoining buildings afire, and flames leaped high into the humid night air.

Still the two men battled on, ignoring the spreading conflagration. Slowly but surely, Von Eismann was wearing Ki down, pummeling his defenses and pounding his body, mere flesh and blood no match for hammering steel. Sooner or later Ki would falter, and the Iceman would dispose of him once and for all. Yet even with the possibility of defeat looming in his mind, Ki fought valiantly, taking the mauling punishment while seeking any opening he could find.

Over the crackling rumble of the blaze could now be heard the clanging of bells. A steam pumper, hauled by a brace of galloping horses, swerved into the alley's mouth up ahead, with the intention of taking the narrow lane as a shortcut. It came hurtling toward the struggling combatants, trailing a comet of sparks and pluming boiler smoke behind it.

This the men could not ignore. Its iron tires striking fire from the cobbles, the pumper rushed at them with no way to swerve around them. Almost able to feel the lunging horses breathing against his spine, Ki vaulted toward an inset doorway in the building alongside him. Von Eismann groped for a hole closer to him, as the pumper's lumbering carriage rolled between them, splitting them apart.

Stepping back into the alley in the wake of the pumper, Ki searched frantically for any sign of Von Eismann, his fingers clutching a bunch of *shuriken*. But the Iceman was gone. Raging with frustration, Ki gathered up his fallen knife and *surushin*, and began sprinting toward the fire.

He was nearly to the street when Boucher suddenly came around the corner, spotted him, and approached at a trot.

"Here's where you went," Boucher said as they met. "Lord, you had me worried, Ki. Look at you. Are you okay?"

"Not too bad," Ki responded. "I almost had the bomber, but he slipped away. How's Annette?"

"She's grand, if shaken up," Boucher assured him, turning to walk back to the street. "Almost got the fellow who started it, eh? By the looks of you, he must've been a swamp cat. Who was he, d'you know?"

"I'll know him when I see him again," Ki said. "Come on, let's collect Annette."

The firemen were showing little enthusiasm for battling the blaze, which by now involved an entire block of ramshackle buildings. Steam pumpers puffed and panted steadily, but at nowhere near capacity, and firemen were concentrating only on keeping the flames from spreading to the north, which might happen if they jumped the street. But there was little wind, and what there was carried the smoke toward the levee.

A uniformed police captain and a fire battalion chief stood by, arms crossed, smiling.

Ki and Boucher located Annette, and Boucher insisted that Ki report the bomber's getaway. Again, Ki responded vaguely when questioned about identifying the culprit.

As they departed the scene of the carnage, Annette remarked to Boucher on the lackadaisical efforts of the firefighters.

"Ah, it's a rare opportunity to remove local rat holes," Boucher replied. "Now the vermin will have fewer burrows."

"Smoke makes my eyes water," Ki said. "Let's find out how the others made out."

Chapter 11

The manager looked scandalized when Ki, Annette, and Boucher arrived at the Negresco. The appearance of a pair of shabby derelicts and a shameless trollop was a blotch on the reputation of his prestigious and proper establishment; and worse, he recognized two of them as patrons he'd checked in himself.

But the manager was in no shape to protest. He was already apoplectic over the way his majestic lobby had become a parade ground for bourgeois police. In uniform and mufti, conversing vulgarly in various languages, patrolmen and department hacks kept streaming to and from the hotel's courtyard and Suite 124.

Moving with the flow, the three overheard enough to learn that Donetian Pradier had been detained, but had slipped custody while en route to Chief Goudron's office.

Goudron, no longer needing to be at his office, had retired to the comfort of his private rooms, which by now had taken on the air of a makeshift headquarters. Jessie was with him, having been awakened and notified when Goudron had returned; and to nobody's overt surprise, that meant Captain Thorpe was seated there too.

Goudron was steaming, barking orders and chewing out subordinates, eyes flashing in a heads-will-roll manner. Hearing from Boucher that René Duvin was dead and uncounted thugs were burned out of their dens did little to restore his good humor. He confirmed Donetian Pradier's escape, and bitterly reproached himself.

"For what inane reason did I ever tell that driver to take a long route with *that* one?" he lamented. "I gave him time to overpower his escorts and vanish, only because I wished time to get warrants and such insanities!"

"A pity Duvin is dead," Jessie commented. "Now our questions will have to wait until Pradier is recaptured."

"Don't hold your breath for that, Mam'selle Starbuck. The man knows the city and many people, and is adept at survival. Still, we'll go through the motions." Goudron looked at each of them in turn, then sighed. "Boucher, you stay. But the rest of you, please get to bed and rest. I'll see you are informed should anything more develop."

"The best suggestion I've heard in hours," Jessie said, stifling a yawn as she moved toward the door.

114

Captain Thorpe, grinning somewhat abashedly, trailed after her.

Just to be discreet, Ki and Annette remained and chitchatted a few minutes, then bade each other good night. They went upstairs to the second floor, and Annette didn't mince around, but steered Ki directly into her room. She locked the door while Ki lit the gas jet, then crossed to him.

Palming her chin, Ki turned her to face the softly glowing lamp. "Your bruises are almost gone."

"But my mouth is still tender," she replied with a coy smile. "I must be careful when it makes love to you."

"Which won't be just yet. We're both a mess."

"Ah, this magnificent hotel has provided a huge tub for bathing. Large enough for two." Taking Ki by the hand into the adjoining bathroom, she showed him the great, clawfooted porcelain vat of a tub. "You see?" she declared cheerily, and bent to plug in the stopper.

"I see, all right," Ki said, admiring the view.

She twisted the taps, watched the water surge into the tub for a moment, then eased back against Ki and hugged him. "It'll take a while to fill, but . . . *incroyable!*"

"What is? The hotel's indoor plumbing?" Ki asked, only to become suddenly aware that deft fingers had unbuttoned his fly and were rummaging inside the crotch of his jeans.

"No, *your* plumbing," Annette giggled, using her free hand to unknot his *surushin* belt and tug down his pants.

"Wait," he protested, "we haven't washed yet."

115

"The scent of a man who's exerted himself, who's sweated, is very exciting," she murmured, kneeling before him. "Here I will wash with my tongue."

Her lips parted wide, the tip of her tongue flicking across them, making them glisten wetly in the warm light. Then they slowly enclosed the bulbous crown of his swiftly growing erection, and her tongue circled its coronal ridge, tasting, savoring. Gradually she began to work more of his thickening shaft into her mouth, drawing it deeper as it lengthened.

Tentatively at first, then increasingly swiftly, she bobbed her head up and down along the sensitive column, her cheeks hollowing, her lips moist and clutching, yet light and demanding.

She paused momentarily and withdrew her mouth, gazing up with dark, passion-wide eyes. "I drink you now, and we share the tub. When we've finished, you'll be ready to return many pleasures."

She engulfed him tightly with her sensuous mouth again, drawing strongly on him, her head moving faster and faster, her slender fingers teasing his throbbing scrotum with their nails. Her throat vibrated with moans of delight, and then, despite his yearning for this to continue, Ki could not restrain himself. She drew him deep into her mouth as the hot spurting began, and swallowed eagerly, wantonly draining him to total exhaustion.

Almost with reluctance, she released his flagging manhood and rose to her feet. Her face was flushed and her tongue glided across her sultry lips, as she worked his vest and shirt off, stripping him entirely naked.

"We're going to get into the water and bathe each

other now," she whispered, kissing his bare chest. "Then we'll get into bed, and you will be lovely and hard for me again. You will be my first real lover, Ki!"

"Your lover, I think, will be asleep."

"I'll find a way to keep you awake," she replied with a coquettish smile. "I know a few tricks."

The bath water was warm, inviting lethargy, and they explored each other in the tub for a long time, breathing the spicy scent of the oil that Annette had discovered in a cabinet. Eventually the water cooled and, deciding to get out, they dried each other with fluffy jacquard towels.

Then Annette led Ki to the plump oversized bed, and she showed him the tricks she had promised...

★

Chapter 12

Next morning, Jessie, Ki, and Annette rode in a carriage to New Orleans' Hotel de Ville, the city hall. When they entered Goudron's office in the fortresslike stone complex, they could readily understand why he'd prefer to run operations from his suite.

The office floor was out of sight under tossed and crumpled papers. Plates that had held sandwiches perched everywhere, as did cups and saucers; and a heavy, acrid pall of cigar smoke drifted low on air currents. Assorted police came and went, their faces showing lack of rest or shaves. Maps were strewn on tables. Some men tried to nap while others resorted to coffee to stay awake, or conducted what sounded like several conversations at once.

Chief Goudron presided over all, seated in a swivel chair at a littered rolltop desk. Facing him in a semicircle of other chairs were some older, authoritative-looking men wearing Navy and Coast Guard uniforms. Captain Thorpe, who'd left Jessie at dawn to return to the *Evangeline,* was present in civilian clothes; and Colin Moran's blocky features looked unusually drawn and somber under his bowler hat.

The new arrivals were beckoned to join them. Chairs were produced, introductions were made. Interest seemed to focus on Annette, for reasons other than her tousled appearance.

"We haven't located Donetian Pradier yet," Goudron began, "but our investigations, we believe, have uncovered a line on the river pirates. They're hiding west of here, somewhere deep in Cajun country, and we're hoping, Mam'selle de Londres, you might have some idea what they're up to."

"Simple," she replied promptly. "They're up to their necks in swamps, snakes, and 'gators. They must be; they're not Cajun. If you're implying they are, you don't know us."

"If I gave that impression, mam'selle, I apologize."

"He does have a good question," Jessie said, to help mollify the indignant girl. "The area's too far, too remote to be practical as a hideout for river raiders. And it's too undeveloped to be valuable. The sugar cane, salt, and sulfur there are more costly to steal than they're worth."

"Well, if there's no motive for raiders to be there, maybe they aren't," Ki said. "Maybe the information's wrong."

"M'sieu! All night my clerks were studying Pradier's invoices, and these documents which M'sieu Moran, ah, borrowed for us." Goudron riffled a massive stack of records on his desk. "As Mam'selle Starbuck suggested, bulk supplies were sent regularly westward. To different ports, to be sure, but always westward into the bayous."

Moran nodded. "Aye, and always shipped there by the Continental Express Company, consigned by none other than Thomas Sykes. And don't forget, Ki, the colleen herself has a tragic tale that confirms such men are there."

"They were there when I left, I know," Annette said, grim with memory. "Outsiders who began appearing nearly two years ago, a few at first, then many. All were thugs, fugitives, killers, regardless of their blood; Negroes or Creeks or Anglos running from whatever bad things they'd done. They were elusive, hiding themselves, coming to a settlement only when they wanted liquor. When they would get drunk, they would brag of regaining lost lands, driving the Americans out. But they only made war on us, on my village, on my family."

Thorpe growled, "Scurvy gutter scum, I know their sort, boasting of bravery but preying on the weak." Then, as an afterthought, he turned to a Navy captain and asked, "What if they tried—not that they really could—but what if they tried to grab control of those bayous?"

The captain glanced at his counterpart from the Coast Guard, shrugged, and answered, "It'd be a blister to fight. Our cavalry and infantry would bog down in the swamps, and so would our ships of the line. Any craft larger than a picket boat would get stuck fast aground in those channels."

"Jean Lafitte's ships were not small, and they sailed as they pleased," Annette reminded him firmly.

The captain snorted. *"That* pirate!"

"He was a privateer, not a pirate."

"He was one of your Frenchies, and knew every twisting puddle of the bayous. He's also been dead for over fifty years, my dear, and's not much good at navigating now."

"Ah, but what he may've left behind!" she countered. "In my home parish is Orange Island, home of Jean Lafitte's brother-in-law. Lafitte was known to take sanctuary there, and some of our elders claim he buried his plunder there. Millions of dollars in gold and silver and precious jewels!"

"Egad, are you suggesting these drunken swine are engaged in a fortune hunt, that along with whiskey, they can buy maps at every Cajun trading post?"

Jessie laughed, interjecting, "No, those are on offer in the gentlemen's clubs of London and Paris and New York. Still, you must admit Annette's raised a possibility."

"But of course!" Goudron slapped his hand on the desk. "Whether or not the treasure exists, its vision alone would lure such *vauriens*—and more than a few wealthy men of Donetian Pradier's ilk. They'd murder and destroy, they'd torture their own grandmothers, for a crack at that prize."

"Well, damn, Orange Island is as good a place as any to start hunting these raiders," Thorpe declared. "We'd get more lost than ol' Jean's treasure, though, without some flatboats or pirogues and guides who know the bayous."

121

The Coast Guard officer spoke up skeptically. "Don't count on local help. Cajuns distrust civil authorities."

"We distrust *all* outsiders," Annette cut in.

"No doubt with reason," Goudron agreed. "However, now we must ask their help. Would they listen to you?"

"Possibly," she replied after some consideration. "My father would, even knowing I was speaking for outsiders."

"Fine. Now the quickest and easiest way to your father would be to go 'round to the bayous by sea."

"Captain Thorpe—"

"Captain Thorpe would be the first to admit, Mam'selle, that sternwheelers are not for offshore voyages." Goudron swiveled in his chair and regarded the officers. "So that is one reason why I asked the government here. Gentlemen?"

Again there was an exchange of glances; this time time the captain indicated that the Coast Guard captain should do the talking. He said, "We're willing to deploy a revenue cutter, and the Navy will assign a squad. Understand, however, that our cooperation has strict limits. Last month a government packet, its entire crew and cargo of ordnance and materiel, disappeared on the bayous without a trace. We've no intention of risking another vessel."

"As it is, we're having to lay this on as a training exercise," the captain added. "I've no authorization to muster an expeditionary force."

"Call it whatever suits you, but let's not dawdle any longer," Jessie said. "How soon can we sail?"

The Coast Guardsman shook his head. "I'm sorry,

Miss Starbuck, but regulations forbid unnecessary females aboard."

"Then lie to yourself that I'm male!"

"I'm not that good a liar, ma'am," he demurred, appraising her tight-fitting shirt and jeans.

"Bah!" Annette stamped her foot angrily. "If Miss Starbuck can't go, I won't go. And if I remain, there's no point in your Navy going, for the Cajun men will steal your little boats while the Cajun women rape your marines. So!"

"Well . . . perhaps in a big, heavy coat. We don't require body searches," the Coast Guardsman muttered, capitulating.

And then he, the Navy captain, and Chief Goudron together sighed the sigh of men plagued by women.

Chapter 13

The Gulf of Mexico was restless, with rollers of more than four feet tossing the revenue cutter around like a chip of wood. Built for speed and maneuverability rather than easy riding, it was some fifty feet long, with a beam of little more than a quarter of that. It bristled with small arms, and mounted a four-pounder forward. Powerful steam engines sent it knifing through the unruly seas at a steady clip. But if the weather held, the Coast Guard officers in command estimated at least two and more likely three days to pass Terrebonne Parish and veer north up the open lakes toward the western reaches of St. Martin Parish.

Nobody believed for a moment that the weather, deceptively calm, was going to hold. Something yet far to the south was prodding the sea air to life. Energy was coalescing in the thin gauzy sky, building a malignant force that would escalate into a wind-lashing squall.

Sea birds were riding the currents to land; shrimp boat sails billowed as they headed for port. On this night, only the cutter was making for the open sea.

Captain Thorpe, no blue-water sailor, confided to Jessie that the Coast Guard must be mad. But the crew operating the cutter seemed to see nothing out of the ordinary in their venture. The stokers never seemed to miss the flaming maws of the fireboxes as they rhythmically shoveled coal, no matter the cant of the deckplates under their feet. On the other hand, the rest of the company, including six Marines under the command of a Lieutenant Lysander, were seasick.

The first rain, pushed by strong southerly gusts, struck as the cutter turned inland, heading for the broad inland waterway that would lead to St. Martin Parish.

Low-lying fingers of land separated the interconnecting lakes, and the land was more illusion than reality, being more of a thick silt that sustained tall grasses and stands of live oaks and gum trees. Semitropical growth bloomed in profusion, and birds were abundant, some with brilliant plumage, some so matched to their surroundings that they were impossible to see when roosting. Alligators sunned themselves along the banks or swam like half-submerged logs; and from the soggy land came the continuous grunting of wild hogs and the occasional scream of a cat.

In the predawn grayness of the third day, they caught fleeting glimpses of light, marking isolated shacks or a few clustered into a settlement.

The one thing totally missing was the sight of a human being.

In the tiny wheelhouse, Annette stood alongside the helmsman and pointed out which channels to follow. To all the others, one stretch of water looked exactly like another, but the Cajun girl seemed to know where she was, and it was seldom necessary for her to ask them to reverse and try another dark, brackish course.

Eventually they came to a basin about a hundred yards across. Daybreak starkly revealed a cluster of fishing shacks and a rickety wharf to which several pirogues and skiffs were tied, bobbing on the wind-chopped water.

"Not here," she cautioned. "This boat would take the dock away. There, to your left. The oaks with big limbs hanging over the water. You can moor to them without becoming a stuck. No anchors."

"They're out there," Thorpe muttered. "But where?"

"Word was sent," she assured him. "They'll have been expecting us since last night."

"I see no telegraph wires," Lieutenant Lysander commented.

The Cajun girl merely smiled. A sailor was reaching up to knot a mooring line to the low-hanging branch of an immense live oak. Spanish moss bearded the venerable tree. Annette sprang onto the limb, which was a good two feet thick, and whispered, "I'll call to you in a few minutes."

Then she disappeared into the veil of moss.

"Spooky," Lieutenant Lysander said, and the helmsman grunted agreement. "One second she's there, then poof!"

126

Annette reappeared just as stunningly, crouching, her face poking pertly through the silver-gray moss. "It is good. My father is nearby, and has been sent for. Few people remember me; I left just after we moved here. But those that do remember me have agreed to talk to the leaders."

Captain Thorpe and the senior Marine and Coast Guard officers figured they qualified. One by one they clambered onto the slippery tree limb and managed to make it to shore without tumbling into the water. Annette's bare feet hardly seemed to touch the smooth bark.

Waiting until the last of them had gone, Jessie shucked her boots and, together with Ki, followed without a sound. Although she wanted to avoid squabbling with the federal support party, she had no intention of being excluded from the plotting. After all, wasn't she the rightful owner of the steamboat that had been attacked, launching this entire bloody affair?

By now the wind had risen to a buffeting wail, hurling sheets of rain at her and Ki. The limb was as slick as if it had been waxed, and twice she would have been blown off, if Ki hadn't been behind her with a supporting hand. They dropped to the spongy bank, where liquid earth squished up between her toes. Ignoring the clammy sensation, Jessie accompanied Ki as they headed after the others, who were just entering one of the small, spartan cabins of swamp cypress that faced the dock. The cabin door closed before they reached it, so they knocked politely and went in.

To her relief, Jessie got nothing worse than scowls from the officers, which were more than balanced by a wink from Captain Thorpe. At least she assumed it was a wink. He could have been trying to remove a cinder from his eye; the cabin's woodstove was belching out sulfurously stinging smoke.

A blackened kettle of gumbo simmered on the stove top, and from the oven filtered the odor of baking bread. A silent older woman, evidently some distant cousin of Annette's, was frying chunks of fresh hog meat in a heavily crusted iron skillet. Outside, the storm was making thunder on the leaky roof, and punching at the sideboards.

The door burst open and three Cajun men, shaking themselves like wet terriers, crowded inside. One was carrying two fat, fresh-caught bass, and he was grinning expectantly.

"Papa!" Babbling happily in Cajun patois, Annette embraced the man, kissing his craggy, scruffily bearded face. Although he favored his right leg, he hoisted his daughter in strong, long-muscled arms, and spun her about so vigorously that his fish got tossed across the room.

"I feared you'd forgotten me," he said when he finally let Annette down. "When young'uns go away from here, they usually stay away."

"Forget? Never, I forget! Once I dreamed you had sickened and died from your wounds, and I almost came back."

"These scratches, hah! Baptiste de Londres, he thrives on mere scratches." He patted the sheath of the bowie-style knife on his belt, a wicked glint to his eye. "But others died and more will yet, 'less we scratch some heads from their necks." He eyed the strangers meaningfully then, adding, "Even help from *les Americains* is welcome. Past due!"

During the introductions, Lieutenant Lysander surprised everyone by responding in flawless Canadian French.

"State of Maine, myself," he explained. "Kennebunkport. We get a lot of Canucks there, summers."

Switching again to Canadian French, Lysander inquired why Baptiste felt they were late in coming, since they were not exactly welcome at any time. He listened thoughtfully to the Cajun reply, and then said to the others, "Well, now. This fellow's located that lost Navy packet, about three hours from here. Moored at some rundown island plantation, nice as you please, the ordnance and cargo still intact. He doesn't know what for."

"And the crew?" the Coast Guard officer demanded.

"Seems they're still alive, most of them, but not in prime shape. They and some Cajuns, totaling about twenty in all, are stuck in some sort of prison camp out there, doing the dirty work for the fellows who nabbed them. There's another boat there too, an old sidewheel paddleboat. Don't know if Uncle Sam's missing one of them, do you?"

"No, it'd have to be civilian." The Coast Guardsman opened a heavy chart case and unrolled its tightly curled maps, finding room on the uneven floorboards to spread them out. "All right, where are we? And where are *they?*"

This set off a noisy debate in patois, which none of the visitors could follow. Annette, as the only one conversant in all the tongues in use, became official interpreter, pointing out channels and islands and the like. But their Cajun hosts, while knowing every soaked inch of four or five parishes, were nonetheless baffled by the charts, for they'd never seen their territory laid out from a bird's-eye view. They puzzled and debated, calling sites by everything except what had been labeled by the cartographers, and this went on for over an hour, until a break was ordered.

The gumbo was dished out in bowls and mugs, and it almost created another rumpus. Made with crawfish, shrimp, sea bass, and a variety of vegetables, the gumbo's stock had been liberally fortified with a pepper sauce hot enough to braze the plates of a steam boiler. The result was a hasty boardinghouse scramble for chunks of fresh bread and pots of hot coffee and jugs of bayou bourbon.

When they settled back to business, one of the first questions came from Lieutenant Lysander. "How many are we facing?"

Baptiste de Londres gave a shrug and consulted with the men who had come in with him. Annette interpreted the consensus. "Something like sixty or so. But not all in one group, of course. They'll be in many places, small groups, a dozen or so to each."

"Damn! Outnumbered for sure, and in their swamp."

"Help is coming," she told him. "Friends and relatives, at least eight and possibly more, with knives and boats."

"And I'll bet the upshot is as disorganized as a dogfight," Thorpe predicted grimly to Jessie and Ki. "These Cajuns are hell for fighting, so long as each one runs his own scrap."

"Worry about that when we catch up with the raiders," Ki advised. "If we've got reinforcements, how

130

do we get us and them to this rundown plantation or whatever it is?"

The Coast Guardsman interjected, "That's the ticket! We'll release the prisoners and secure the packet, which will give us plenty more fighting men and the weapons for them."

"The packet's one thing, but I wouldn't rely too much on those men, not if they're in weakened condition. They may be more of a hindrance than a help, but I agree, that's where we should head." Jessie glanced ceilingward, as though gazing at the sky. "The storm will help cover our approach, too."

Lieutenant Lysander nodded. "If the Cajuns can get here by sundown, we can try moving in on that damned island and points close by. Be in position to go ashore by midnight. Let me palaver some more, and see what we can come up with."

In French again, the lieutenant began conversing with Annette and the Cajun men. Captain Thorpe listened intently, trying to get the gist of it. The Coast Guard officer simply gave up, and knelt to consult his charts. Jessie and Ki walked out onto the front porch, which was protected from the downpour.

They stood watching the dark bayou waters being peppered with warm, salty raindrops. Mists were rising, drifting, alternately concealing and revealing the revenue cutter a hundred feet away. They became aware of furtive shadows moving through the undergrowth, and from the mists came swarthy men who silently slipped ashore and off into the jungle growth, paying them no heed.

Thoughtfully, Ki scuffed his foot against the porch's wet wood. "Jessie, what we're up against is too big for Pradier. This is a cartel show, the Iceman showing up proves that much."

"And too big to be something as nebulous as scrounging for Jean Lafitte's treasure. But whatever Von Eismann is up to, I don't think this motley bunch of renegades will give him much loyalty. If they hold together, it'll be Pradier who does the holding. Holding . . . Ki, it makes me wonder . . ."

"It makes me remember. What Annette said—you know, about those men bragging how they'd get hold of the bayous."

"What if it's not nonsense? What if the cartel's been slowly infiltrating men with greed for booty or a grudge against America? The cartel's been functioning for over a century; it wouldn't mind if it took a few decades to gradually build a ragtag army of desperadoes and lowlifes, until eventually it could rise and seize control."

"It'd have its own state, Jessie, and it would be virtually impossible to retake. A country of fugitives with a squeeze on our jugular, the Mississippi—and miles of coastline on the Gulf of Mexico for smuggling dope and arms or whatever."

"And by grabbing a vast portion of the Louisiana Purchase, the cartel would present a staggering loss to the United States throughout the world. Ki, it's just the sort of show those madmen would love to pull off."

At that moment, Lieutenant Lysander poked his head out the doorway and said, "We've got it worked out as best we can. See what you think."

They walked inside and were shown a crudely drawn map of Orange Island, which was shaped roughly like

132

a deformed crookneck squash. At its highest point it was no more than fifty feet above the bayou, being a thin layer of fertile earth formed over countless eons atop a salt dome.

Baptiste de Londres retrieved the map and sketched on its backside with a thick, stubby pencil. The short time with his English-speaking visitors had brought back his ability to communicate more or less fluently in that tongue, so Annette's translations ended.

"The steamers here," he said, pointing to the cove formed by the hook. "The captives here, south, close to the bayou, nine hundred, a thousand yards. All hard earth, no wet marsh. Old cane fields. Big house, here."

The plan of attack was, on its face, effective. It called for most of the Marines to stay with the cutter, which would bring them offshore of the island, as close as possible to the prisoners. Then a landing party would move into position and storm the compound. Once the prisoners were safe, the party would cross the island and capture the two boats.

Ki sighed inwardly, knowing it wouldn't work.

"How are the prisoners kept?" Jessie wanted to know. "What about the guards?"

"The compound is barbed-wire fence, and there are only a few guards, because the poor blighters are in rough shape," Lieutenant Lysander answered. "Frankly, I'm more concerned about those boats, particularly the packet with its big arsenal. De Londres swears there's only a skeleton crew on it, and just a couple of boiler tenders on the sidewheeler. How to take them, and when, that's what's got me scratching my head."

"Why?" Ki asked. "A small boarding team—"

"Even at night, with mists, we'd have the odds stacked against us, climbing aboard the packet. Got to figure these fellows we're after have got them mined. Maybe prisoners aboard, too."

Thorpe said, "The cutter could blockade the cove."

"Except that the cutter will have to be standing well off, so it can give support all around the lake."

"Well, then, how can we land, Lieutenant?"

"The same way the locals will, in pirogues and skiffs. We'll string them on lines behind the cutter. Then they drop off along the island perimeter, and we all slip ashore."

Ki frowned, feeling uneasy. "Tell me about the big house."

"Oh, it's only a shell," Annette said, shrugging. "It was a mansion, maybe a hundred years old. Most of the walls stand, though some of the roof's rotted in on the upper floor, and the chimney's still there. That's all."

"How close would it be to the cove?"

She thought for a moment. "Perhaps three hundred yards in a straight line, but there is no straight line. It's the highest part of the island, and the wagon trail to the landing wanders. Now there's just new growth, very thick." She surveyed Ki's physique and added, "A panther of a man like you might get through it in a half hour, with a machete. It could not be done in less."

"A half hour will do," Ki said with a grin.

Lysander snapped, "Do for what, mister?"

"To get there and set up the diversion, Lieutenant."

"What diversion? The plan calls for no diversion!"

134

Ki stopped. He stopped talking, stopped moving, stopped even looking as though he might do such actions, and waited a long second for the sense of confrontation to melt away. Then he gave Lieutenant Lysander a calm yet controlled smile.

"A diversion, a noisy one, will let you attack the compound while the guards are distracted. Also, that old ruin would be a natural spot for the raiders to hole up in, and I might catch a lot of them with their pants down."

"And if you get caught? Or killed?"

"Give me a half-hour start after you land your men, Lieutenant," Ki urged. "If I don't make it, then it's simple—the plan has no diversion."

Lysander mulled over the risks, muttering. "Sixty of them skulking around, against six Marines, eleven Cajuns—"

"Twelve," Annette interrupted. "Including me."

Distracted, he glared. "My men are veterans."

"Who are dressed in pretty uniforms that'll make grand targets," Annette retorted. "I'm a veteran of the bayous. I won't get shot like a tropical bird in full plumage."

Lysander felt stung, but decided to forgo the issue of the Cajun count. "My men, me, one civvy—"

"Two," Jessie chimed in.

"You're not a Cajun, you're a lady!"

"She's a crack shot and sturdy under fire," Thorpe declared. "I'll vouch for that. Don't say such a fool thing."

"You need all the *men* you can get," she added.

"That's my point," Lysander objected. "I can't afford to detail any of my men to go with Ki."

"I don't want any. Send your men crashing through the jungle, and the raiders will scatter like rabbits," Ki argued. "What I need is a real sneaky Cajun as guide."

Lysander grumbled, feeling the weight of responsibility and the length of the odds. Reluctantly he agreed. "I can't stop you, so you may as well try it."

"I'll need a few items from your supplies, too."

"Sure, sure, whatever catches your fancy."

"And I'll see what the natives might have on hand," Ki added. Motioning Annette away from the group, he spoke urgently to her. They went out the door and into the rain.

The others continued to refine the plan.

Chapter 14

It was a weird-looking flotilla that finally nosed out into the creek and made for distant Orange Island.

On a clear day there would have been at least another hour of sunlight; but the clouds, scudding along with their cargo of rain and wind, brought only early twilight. The surface of the bayou was roiling, its waters pelleted with fat droplets spearing down through the shifting mists.

The sounds of nature completely muffled the chugging of the cutter's engine as it eased its way through a serpentine maze of creeks, passing ghostlike beneath gray-bearded live oaks and dropping cypress boughs. Behind the cutter stretched a variety of pirogues and *bateaux*—thin, flat-bottomed boats which drew barely a few inches of water, and could be poled directly through the stands of swamp grasses.

In these, armed with pistols, knives, swords, throwing axes, and even long blacksnake whips, rode the vengeance-seeking kinfolk and friends of Annette de Londres. Her father, piloting, rode the cutter, along with Jessie, Captain Thorpe, and Lieutenant Lysander and his squad.

Bobbing along in the rearmost boat, Ki kept company with a stocky, one-eyed Cajun who called himself Bonhomme Richard. His guide, Annette had assured Ki, was not only the sneakiest of the men available, but could also speak sufficient English for Ki to be able to work alone with him. After he'd heard Bonhomme recount a few of his brave exploits, Ki became convinced that anyone able to concoct such patent hokum was the type of imaginative rascal he needed.

Yet, so far, Ki had refused to disclose any details of his plan in advance, and what he had in mind had left Bonhomme, as well as the others, utterly mystified. Between the two of them, however, they'd collected in the boat an impressive arsenal: two .44-40 Winchesters and a Colt of the same caliber, two machetes, a handful of cheroots, oilskin packets of gunpowder and detonator caps, a short case of dynamite, a coil of fuse, pieces of rawhide and rope, and a squat bow and a quiver of arrows, as well as a skein of fishing line.

Some of these things belonged to Bonhomme. Most were contributed by Ki; and the reason he wouldn't confide how he planned to use them was that he couldn't. He had no specific plan; he'd merely confiscated anything that looked as if it might be useful.

Ki wasn't sure just where they were in relation to

the island, but Bonhomme Richard was. The Cajun slipped the towline and began to pole the bateau toward shore. He understood where they wanted to go, and Ki had every confidence that they would go exactly where Bonhomme planned.

Shortly thereafter, other flatboats and pirogues cut loose in similar maneuvers. They were joined by dinghies from the cutter; Baptiste, Jessie, Thorpe, and Lieutenant Lysander were in the last dinghy to leave. Behind them, the cutter withdrew to cruise offshore until needed, with only the Coast Guard crew to man her.

The various boats grounded along a wide stretch of shoreline without raising an alarm. Merging on the beach, the team immediately pushed on with no more than an exchange of flinty smiles, as comment upon the fact that they were now on enemy soil. The idea was to take one of the numerous trails across the island, from the northernmost point of the neck to the section where it began to belly out, where the cane fields had grown long ago. Communication was by touch and brief, low calls that were swept away by the wind; but communication was kept to a minimum, for fear of alerting the raiders. And should they meet any raiders, the order was simple: Kill quietly.

As Baptiste had told his men, "When the outsider does whatever it is he'll do, he'll make much noise. Then we will make plenty of noise of our own. Like savages."

The group marched almost at double-time, paced ten yards apart, except for the point man, who kept three times that distance ahead. Baptiste was a pointman. He liked the position, and was as adept at guiding as anyone; and because of his game leg, he was generally not as quiet as the others, so it was best to have him out in front, away from the main body.

But if the Cajun was a little noisier, that didn't stop his leg from setting a mean pace. The team made excellent time keeping up with his strides, remaining vigilant, weapons at the ready.

They were filing through a slope of man-high grass when Baptiste dropped to the muddy earth. The team behind him dove for cover, and waited. Baptiste slipped forward, disappeared for a couple of minutes, then eased back to where his daughter, Jessie, and Thorpe were hiding.

On his belly, he whispered, "Men coming, on the path."

"How many?" Jessica asked.

He gave a little shrug. "A dozen or so. I don't think they're looking for us; they move too noisy. But they *are* moving this way."

"But only a dozen..." Thorpe's eyes glinted. "Hell, the odds are with us."

"Ah, but silence is not," Annette warned. "We—"

Then bodies came thrashing along the grass-lined trail. Jessie could make out the hazy outlines of men bundled against the driving rain. Rifle stocks were being swung to mash the grass aside, and in a matter of seconds the raiders would strike one of them, and then the rifles would be used more conventionally.

Impetuously, Baptiste didn't wait for that to happen. There was the sigh of a hand against fabric, then the glint of his knife arcing upward to bury itself in the nearest man's chest. Thorpe was launching a silencing tackle at the next man in line, even as the first was flopping in a heap, gurgling quietly to himself. But Thorpe was an instant too late. The third man, realizing something was wrong, gave out a spontaneous yelp—which was choked off by a lung-piercing stab, as Annette landed atop him.

Jessie, slitting the throat of yet another raider, sensed the damage that had been done by that yell. The more men they could take quietly, simultaneously, the better their odds against the rest. That was why she'd stabbed her victim through the side of the neck and ripped outward, the way Ki had trained her; the more common method of slicing from ear to ear would have allowed the man one last, loud shout. And although Jessie found killing distasteful to the point of nausea sometimes, she felt no mercy, no pity for this cartel riffraff, only an implacable determination that if it must be done, she would do it right.

Baptiste had counted correctly. There had been twelve raiders, tightly packed, and weary from slogging from wherever they'd been to wherever they were going. And Jessie had sensed correctly; the rest of the raiders pulled up in confusion in response to that one yell.

But it was short affair, over almost as soon as it began. The other Cajuns had slithered noiselessly through the grass in a two-pronged flanking action, and were already pouncing from the trail's sides as the raiders started shouting and raising their weapons. It became a one-on-one melee, and the moment's shouting was quickly stilled.

The raiders lay sprawled, blood flowing like the rainwater along the path's channel. Jessie spoke to

Lysander and Baptiste about the bodies; they nodded, and split up to swiftly check their respective groups and follow her advice.

The response was a furious scramble, as corpses and weapons were slung away from the trail. Then the grass was hastily bunched up in the trampled undergrowth, forming a makeshift fence to further cloak the scene of action. It wouldn't have fooled even a blind man for more than ten minutes—but those ten minutes could make a great deal of difference.

"How are we?" Jessie asked Lysander when he passed again. "Anyone hurt?"

"Two of my men. Very minor, a scalp wound and a laceration. And one of the Cajuns got kicked in the, uh—"

"Yes, I imagine that would hurt."

Re-forming their line, they moved on swiftly along the path toward the spine of the island, to put as much distance between them and the dead as possible. The trail snaked over the shallow ridgeline and descended crookedly through a marshy patch of bracken. Gamely the team struggled, their clothes soggy and leaden and seeming to weigh them down that much more in the soupy terrain. They reached the deserted cane fields, now grown wild with a vengeance.

Eventually Baptiste halted in the dense undergrowth, beyond which, he said, a clearing of perhaps two acres had been hewn out. "The prisoners," he whispered, pointing.

Rising, peering through the dripping foliage, they found themselves fifty to sixty feet from a barbed-wire entanglement. It enclosed more than an acre that they could see, and an unknown area sloping downhill

142

away from them. Despite the lashing rain, small cook-fires were burning, and by their wavering light it was possible to see the outlines of men, a lot of them limping, some using crutches, all moving with the numbed slowness of the sick and injured amid make-shift shelters of wood and canvas.

"Swamp fever's probably done more to lay the poor bastards low than anything else," Captain Thorpe muttered. "Not many guards in sight; I'd hazard fewer than the last set."

Annette gestured to an indistinct dark shape near one of the fence corners. "Look, that big gun, there. It's outside the wire, set up to cover the prisoners."

"A Gatling gun." Jessie, recognizing the distinctive outline of the .51-caliber death machine, felt a shiver of dread up her spine. "Good chance they figure to mow down the prisoners at the first hint of trouble. We'll have to take it out quietly, before Ki pops the cork."

Lieutenant Lysander shook his head. "We may not have time. Besides, there are enough rifles among us for each man to pick himself a guard, and the rest to target that Gatling."

"We can't see if there are more Gatlings posted down at the other end, and it's likely there are," Jessie countered.

"*Mais oui*," Baptiste agreed. "The machines we must stop now. Then our volleys will kill the guards."

Wound up after the victorious skirmish on the trail, the lieutenant lusted for more swift, decisive battle; yet his training and common sense cautioned that they were right.

He started slithering forward through the thicket,

143

his short belt-knife clenched in his teeth, the front of his uniform covered with slime. Watching him, Jessie judged that he was better than fair at crawling, but only the saving grace of the lush foliage was protecting his butt.

Evidently Baptiste was of the same opinion. Signaling to one of the Cajun men who'd been with him in the cabin, Baptiste and the other man began creeping after Lysander, blades in hand.

All three vanished from view. Nothing happened for the next few minutes, the only sound being that of the gusty rain. The black outline of the Gatling gunner then shifted, and he called out in a voice more curious than suspicious.

No answer. Another minute or two passed.

The gunner called again, louder and more querulously. Suddenly his voice choked off as another dark shape seemed to rise and merge with his silhouette.

The best that Jessie could discern from the strange shadow-dancing was that Lysander was pressing close behind the gunner, holding him by the neck. The gunner's wide hat had tipped askew with his head, his boots tapping on the edge of the low platform, while he shuddered convulsively in Lysander's grip. Then Lysander released him and propped him laxly behind the Gatling, so that it would appear as if the gunner were still on the job.

Lysander had slain the gunner swiftly and efficiently; he simply hadn't known the man was not alone. What two other guards were doing under the platform was anyone's guess. But before Lysander could position the gunner perfectly, the pair had leaped from underneath and attacked. Unaware that their cohort was dead, they were trying to rescue the man, wrestling him away while pistol-whipping Lysander.

Lysander had fallen off the platform and was struggling on his knees, when Baptiste and the other Cajun charged into the fight. One of the guards kicked Lysander in the head, then pivoted to aim at Baptiste. But Baptiste was closing too fast with his knife, and the guard only had time to block Baptiste's thrust with his gun arm. Baptiste parried, and was curving his knife back underneath the guard's arm for another stab, when his Cajun friend skewered his own blade up under the guard's ribs, and then cut him open all the way to his breastbone. Blood and viscera mushroomed out, the guard toppling backward, mouth and eyes wide open.

Springing aside to avoid the gushing gore, the two Cajuns glanced to where Lysander was dispatching the other guard by using his knee and a neck lock to break the man's spine. There was a *crack!* which Jessie felt more than heard, and then the second guard dropped out of sight to the ground.

Not surprisingly, the six-man scuffle up around the gun platform was not overlooked. A shout went up from inside the compound. Apparently working under some impression that the fight was just another personal row between colleagues, the guards trotted toward the fence, gesturing and yelling to them to cut it out. Then a guard got close enough to see that it was a bit more serious than that, and lunging aside, he brought his carbine up to bear.

Lysander, who'd leaped back up onto the platform, swiveled the Gatling around while fiddling with its intricate release and cocking mechanisms. Putting his academy training as well as a strong right arm into use, Lysander turned the gun's crank and sent the guard reeling with a short burst of fire.

At which point, the Gatling jammed.

The two Cajun men had, for stealth's sake, only taken knives with them. They didn't even have the knives in play, but were also on the platform, trying to help Lysander loosen a malfunctioning breech in the Gatling.

Jessie, realizing that the situation could swiftly degenerate into defeat, straightened with her borrowed Henry rifle, and fired at the first guard that came within her sights. The rest of the team rushed forward through the field, where they had been covering the action. They'd purposely been holding their fire, but now it was obvious that, ready or not, their attack had been triggered, and they had no choice but to carry it through.

And the guards were ready. The Gatling's blasts had galvanized them, sending them diving for cover, kicking and punching the prisoners aside, and opening up a withering barrage of gunfire.

In a few more minutes, Jessie realized, Ki might produce his promised diversion. But in a few more minutes there might not be any more reason to have one.

Of all the damn times for Ki to be on time!

Chapter 15

Ki felt he was late.

He had felt he was late from the moment he and Bonhomme Richard had beached their bateau and he had surveyed the impenetrable climb to the rear of the crumbling mansion. The slope had made him reconsider taking the longer yet easier wagon road, but he'd rejected it as too risky. Annette had recalled the road as being overgrown, but that was from two years ago, and maybe it was being used again. He'd hoped it was; he'd hoped to find the mansion merely decayed, not deserted.

So, splitting the supplies, Ki and Bonhomme rigged loads to each other's backs with rope and rawhide slings, and then set off with machetes swinging. Night clung low to the living, pulsing mass of tangled foliage, thickening the steamy veil of rain and swelling the fetid odors of mold and dank moss.

Ki kept on going, though, knowing that he had to meet a deadline and that he'd fallen behind schedule already. He plodded on, one foot at a time, hacking and chopping alongside Bonhomme, cursing as the plants he'd cut seemed to sprout right up again.

They splashed across a solidly slimed stream, one of the thousands like capillaries on the hill, and then hurried ahead when crashing things wriggled in the stagnant mass.

The incline grew steeper, and they veered slightly off course to avoid the worst of the undergrowth. It was treacherous walking, the ground like gumbo in one spot and then as slippery as black ice in the next, and the sluicing runoffs undermining their footing, threatening to send the men tumbling into the choking depths.

Gamely the men hacked their way to the rolling summit, finding no respite from the storm. Their cumbersome packs, soggy and leaden, kept shifting on their backs, unbalancing them still further as they staggered and slid.

There was a sense of relief when they leveled off on the back acreage of the estate. The way was still rough, formal gardens and cultivated vegetation having gone berserk; but it was nowhere near as tortuous, and the wind was slackening slightly, though the rain still fell in eddies.

Ahead loomed the rear of the mansion, and from this distance Ki could conjure what it must have looked like in its heyday—with a vast ground floor and a roofline beginning above that; with dormer windows projecting on the upper story; and a great square cupola above that, resembling the pilothouse of a river packet. But what Ki liked best was the lamplight now glowing in the windows.

"Looky there," Bonhomme drawled. "Somebody's home."

Ki grinned. "Let's be neighborly and drop in."

Between them and the house were the cabins for the house slaves, and the separate kitchen, all of them in various states of ruin. A couple of the cabins appeared to be used for shelter, and light was showing in an empty window frame of the kitchen. The kitchen was connected to the house by a wide flagstone patio; except for that barren paved section, the surrounding land had flourished with a vengeance, with youngish trees and flowering bushes encroaching to squeeze the very foundations of the buildings.

"We've got to check the kitchen," Ki said. "I don't want our backs to it, once we get across to the house."

Together they began a crouching sprint toward the kitchen, advancing in circuitous stages, dipping from tree to tree, shrub to shrub, continually on the lookout for patrolling men. When they reached the side of the kitchen with the lighted window, they flattened as best they could and edged along until they were beside the broken frame.

Ki glanced over the sill, and instantly dropped. He held up his hand to Bonhomme, two fingers extended.

Bonhomme nodded, and was slipping a knife from its sheath when a touch from Ki halted him. Ki whispered, "That will only take one. The other might shout."

Then, low and slowly, Ki padded up to the corner. Bonhomme followed, wondering what Ki had in mind,

149

as Ki peered out from around the corner, across the stone terrace.

The terrace extended the entire width of the kitchen, and midway along it, what was left of the doorway could be seen. Apparently there wasn't a door any longer, but from the corner's sharp angle, Ki couldn't tell what was going on inside. He concentrated on hearing sounds from the interior, to learn if the men had shifted or were moving.

Bonhomme nudged him, impatient. "Eh?"

Ki felt that instinctive warning in his gut. If they crossed the terrace and were spotted from either the kitchen or the house, they wouldn't have a chance. But there wasn't a peep coming from the kitchen. "We'll hit the doorway, then head for the other side of the house. Me first."

Hunkering low, they dashed across the terrace toward the doorway. A step ahead of Bonhomme, Ki fingered two steel *shuriken* from his vest, twisted leftward, and sprang through the doorway, tossing both disks underhand.

Lounging at a three-legged table were a couple of whiskery, gimlet-eyed pistoleros, playing penny-ante poker. The man facing Ki, on the far side of the table, was yawning as the *shuriken* slashed cleanly through his throat, severing voice box and carotid artery before lodging in his collarbone. He was already dropping, his lifeblood gushing over the discard pile, when his partner abruptly nodded his head forward, the second *shuriken* protruding from the base of his skull where it was joined by the spinal cord.

"*Foutre!*" Bonhomme gasped, peering inside.

Without responding to the Cajun's astonishment,

Ki swiveled on the ball of one foot, darted around Bonhomme, and angled across the rest of the terrace toward the other side of the big house. When he was almost to the bordering strip of massive shrubs, he heard the scuffing of boots behind him. That was either Bonhomme moving to catch up, or somebody else preparing to shoot him in the back. Whichever it was, Ki wasn't going to waste time looking.

He plunged into the overgrown bushes, slid along the flower beds bordering the house, then hunkered down. Bonhomme drew up beside him a second later, panting from exertion.

The Cajun began, "Never before have I seen—"

Ki shushed him with a finger to his lips.

From their position they were able to view what had once been an expanse of lawn. The now waist-high thatch led to the porticoed main entrance, the leaning columns of which framed the gaping front door, its wooden steps now rotted, warped wood. Some great piece of ironmongery, like an overturned pot, bulked nearby.

They were also, from where they hunched, able to see through two window holes from which the glass had long ago disappeared. Inside, what remained of the great hall was swarming with upwards of three dozen of the meanest-looking men Ki had ever seen gathered in one spot. They were arguing and drinking and eating with grubby fingers—which, judging by its appearance, couldn't hurt the food any.

Their hulking shapes were illuminated by several oil lamps. Around them were walls with jagged holes where plaster had once been, an odd assortment of crates and boxes, ceiling timbers fallen to the rotted floor, and the maw of a huge stone fireplace, which was now being used as a trash burner. The exterior of the fireplace was also visible, a giant finger thrusting skyward, leaning against the shattered rooftree.

"A good mule could kick it down," Ki murmured, then indicated the piece of ironmongery. "What's that?"

"Sugar kettle. Cane was boiled down in them back then."

"Must hold about a thousand gallons."

"More."

They returned to studying the scene. The men inside the house seemed to be drunk; some had passed out, and the rest had no interest at all in venturing out in the rain.

So much for security, Ki thought, and returned his attention to the chimney. It poked a good fifty feet up; and except for the fractured remains of the ridgepole against which it leaned, it was a good thirty feet taller than any remaining section of the house. Big chunks of roof lay about what once had been the second-story line.

He thought about it all for a minute, then put a question to Bonhomme. He had to rephrase it several times before his meaning became clear to the Cajun.

"*Oui*, there'd be such a door of iron, to open and remove ashes. It will be rusted, certainly."

"Not for long, Bonhomme. Let's see . . ." Burrowing into their packs, Ki assembled dynamite, caps, black powder, and the fishing line. He looped the coil of slow-burning fuse around his neck, and said, "Show me."

Creeping single file, they eased along the side, trying to stay as concealed as possible in the foliage.

152

A gum tree grew up against the house, and its thick leaves had kept the ground almost dry—which was a blessing, Ki thought, because it was so dark around the base of the chimney that he had to do his work almost solely by feel.

As Bonhomme had predicted, the ash-door was a cast-iron slab about a foot and a half square, and was rusted to its frame. It took a while, and some very quiet cursing, yet with careful scraping and prying with the point of Bonhomme's heavy hunting knife, they were able to pry the door open. The hinges groaned and squealed in protest, but all Ki could do was hope the sounds of wind and the drunken shouting inside the house would conceal the noise. Evidently they did; nobody came.

Having done such deeds often enough before, Ki had no difficulty in forming several sticks of dynamite and packets of gunpowder together. Into the end of the center stick he forced a blasting cap, which he then crimped to the end of a length of fuse. He split the last packet of powder and scattered its contents haphazardly.

Bonhomme, whom Ki had dispatched on a search, was bent over, staggering, as he returned with a hunk of broken garden statuary. Then, as Ki shoved the iron door closed, he leaned the stonework against it. As Ki explained to him, the bomb's force would now be directed inward and upward, and not be dissipated out of doors.

Next, Ki measured off a generous minute's worth of fuse. Bonhomme stood by nervously, even though he had watched Ki practicing in the bateau, testing the fuse to determine its particular burn rate. Ki took

153

from his pocket a sulfur match whose head had been dipped in paraffin to waterproof it, struck it on his thumbnail, and touched it to the fuse. When it sputtered and caught, he made sure it was lying without kinks or loops in a dry patch of ground.

The two then hastened through the shadows to the sugar kettle. Here Ki used a length of fishingline to wrap three dynamite sticks together, set a cap and a half-minute fuse, and carefully eased the bundle under the rim of the kettle. It felt as though it was made of cast iron an inch thick, so as an afterthought he slid a few unfused dynamite charges under the kettle lip, and tucked in a final packet of powder.

He lit the fuse and sparks flew.

"Now let's go—and forget about noise!"

They fled, crashing through the undergrowth for a good hundred feet before crouching behind the thick trunk of a live oak. They waited expectantly. And waited.

"Slower fuse than I thought," Ki muttered.

And waited.

Bonhomme rubbed his hands. "Something is wrong."

Ki said confidently, "Fuses burn in fits and starts. It'll go any second now."

And they waited some more.

"I'll go look," Ki groused. "Cowpats burn faster—"

As if to make up for the delay, the first charge detonated with a terrific, brilliant shock wave. They could see the uppermost section of chimney jump high in the air, break into fragments, and come tumbling down. The fireplace and that entire quarter of the

154

mansion were hurled out across the grounds, the remaining walls, beams, windows, and masonry cycloning up and about. The rest of the roof collapsed in the hole the charges had punched, and fire blossomed through the shattered remains, consuming the old building with avid hunger.

The sugar kettle convulsed, lifting off its stand, jetting smoke and incandescence. The lid blew open, releasing a gout of flame with a dull, strangely hollow roar, accompanied by a ringing clatter as massive chunks of iron shrapneled the area. Some pieces slashed through the thick tropical growth around them, and a few bit deep gouges in nearby trees.

The screams of the dying could not be heard for the first deafening minute or two. But by the suddenly sprouting blaze, Ki saw that the living were staggering, panic-stricken, out into the open. Without pause or preamble, he took up the Winchester and fired round after round, picking off killers before they could kill again. They didn't react for a moment, their faces registering shock and agony as Bonhomme brought the other Winchester into accurate play. Then some of the gunmen responded, unslinging their own weapons and shooting in wide swaths, while others loped for cover, as often as not getting in the way of their own comrades.

Seven raiders went down kicking in those first few seconds, under the roaring smash of the twin Winchesters. Chaos reigned in the shambles of the mansion, death striking in the wink of an eyelash out on the grounds. Images engraved themselves in Ki's brain with the speed of light, never to be forgotten.

The bewildered survivors of the fire, vicious but

155

undisciplined, were badly shot up before they could properly collect their wits. A pair tried to mount a defense, counterattacking Ki and Bonhomme in a crossfire. Others rallied with them.

Bonhomme reacted with Cajun efficiency, mowing both men down with a single short sweep of his Winchester. One of the others, a sawed-off scattergun in hand, was sent spinning by Ki. Another did a nosedive and skidded on his face, and a third rolled over and played dead before he actually died.

Bonhomme's hammer clicked on an empty chamber. With an oath, he reached behind in his pack for the Colt revolver, only to discover there were no more targets to hit. There were only two kinds of men anywhere to be seen: the dead and the dying. Any who were left over had fled.

"C'mon," Ki said, breathing heavily. "Let's move."

The distant crackling of gunfire lent urgency to his words. Hurriedly reslinging their now lighter packs, they headed down the hill on the wagon road, able for some distance to feel heat from the blood-red inferno burning behind them.

Chapter 16

Ki's explosive diversion carried with thunderous intensity, despite the muffling effects of storm and subtropical growth. The burning mansion was equally startling, changing night instantly into day with its fiery hilltop beacon.

Down by the compound, the team had been anticipating just such a distraction and, heartened, sent a tidal wave of bullets into the momentarily stunned guards. The severity of the fusillade caused many of the guards to stop in alarm, dead in their tracks. Others, more experienced in gun battles, sought deeper cover—cover that was not there in the stubble-earthed compound—and a few stumbled, shrieking, dropping weapons to clutch their wounds, while most, perhaps half, regrouped to fire back at the attackers.

The mansion's lambent glow, diffused by the clouds

and a slackening rain, spread over the compound. Its presence seemed to inspire the invaders, who charged, yelling encouragements to one another, triggering a withering stream of lead. On the gun platform, Lieutenant Lysander was stubbornly doctoring the balky Gatling, oblivious to the bullets whipping around him. The guards triggered volley after volley, but were met with a withering spray when he finally fixed the Gatling and began cranking off rounds. The guards wavered, foundering, falling behind the prisoners.

"Get down in there!" Lysander bellowed at the prisoners, who were scrambling about in frantic confusion, trying to help their rescuers rip down the barbed wire. "Get down, I say!" But he was overruled by the prisoners, too.

Then the Gatling jammed again, beyond repair. Cursing it, Lysander jumped down and followed his teammates, plunging through the torn barbed-wire fencing and swarming into the compound.

The team raked the guards, determined to decimate them for their role in brutalizing and enslaving innocent people. But the invaders had hopes and promises to live for, and the guards had nothing but frantic desperation. Kill or be killed!

Jessie, sprinting through a spray of muddy grit raised by the bullets striking around her, answered with a salvo from her .38 that smacked a guard in the chest. The man sank earthward, his grubby clothes dissolving in a pink froth of punctures, his staring eyes sightless, his screaming mouth silent.

Pivoting, firing again, she glimpsed the nearest of the attacking team—it was Annette, face contorted, eyes maniacal, as her agile hands triggered revenge.

Just beyond was Baptiste, proving he was every inch her father, self-reliant and heedless of his own safety as he downed one guard and swiveled to find more. Another three guards were trying for the hills, until the Marines stopped them dead.

They, like Jessie and the rest of the team, were aware that Ki's diversion had been a help. Yet the win could be temporary; the hammering gunfire and ferocious shouts were certain to draw more raiders.

And their win would be costly. Captain Thorpe's left ear was almost torn off by a bullet; howling, incensed, he drilled the offending guard with quick one-handed gunnery, clapping his free hand to his temple to stanch the flow of blood. Baptiste's friend, the Cajun who'd help save Lieutenant Lysander, was hit simultaneously in the right bicep and thigh, and toppled with his duck gun blasting skyward. A ricocheting bullet, almost spent, gutshot a young Marine; he gave a sudden hacking cough and slumped, hands to his belly.

But the guard's losses were greater. Stunned and disorganized from the first, they died to the last man— as bewildered, Jessie hoped, as Annette's family and friends had been when the raiders slaughtered them.

The rain had lightened, swirling and dissipating in hazy currents like a fog, when the fighting died away. Lieutenant Lysander immediately ordered the rescue of the packet boat.

Not everyone went. The gutshot Marine didn't. Annette and Baptiste stayed and took turns applying tourniquets to the wounded Cajun. The other Cajuns refused to go, as well, claiming they knew prisoners who were relatives, but no *Americains* who had packet boats. The twenty-odd prisoners could not. Smiling blearily and dazed by this weird stroke of fortune, they were all pale ghosts of their former selves, flesh stretched tight over bones and chests cadaverously hollow—the effects of digging slavishly for Jean Lafitte's elusive trove.

Lysander and his remaining Marines left for the packet boat. Thorpe, an improvised bandage wrapped around his head and covering his torn ear, wanted to see the packet. Jessie said that she wanted to get to the dock, because the road from the mansion went there, and maybe Ki had taken it.

They marched along a rutted wagon path that serpentined from the ridgeline to the landing. When it got a little lower, it meandered across a brackish marsh, and curved lower until the land flattened and the vegetation became thinner from lack of topsoil. Just about the time Jessie was wondering if the trail would skirt water level, it coiled upward again, right back into the thick of things.

They were emerging from an enclosing morass of parasite-clad trees and plump, fleshy plants when they saw Ki and Bonhomme Richard come around the corner ahead.

Both men were running, and when they stopped and the others closed in around them, Ki panted, "Coming down from the old house, and smacked into them before we knew it."

"Who?" Thorpe asked.

What sounded akin to a stampede of cowboy boots could now be heard approaching the same corner. "Them," Ki answered. "Eighteen, twenty of them. And Pradier."

Lysander started to charge, yelling, "Go get 'em!"

"Not that way," Ki said, grabbing his arm and turning him back toward the trees. "This way. Both sides."

Everyone headed for one or another of the dark shoulders of trees. They poised under cover, unlimbering weapons, as the first of Pradier's gunslicks appeared at the bend.

"Are they after you for blowing up the island?" Jessie said.

"When we met at the landing, I didn't pause to ask. Since we were out-gunned, I thought we'd bring them along to you people. Did my firecracker help you?"

"Made the difference, we took the place. Ki, we *must* stop these men here. The ones at the compound won't be able to."

Evidently the men were assuming that Ki and Bonhomme were pushing on along the trail in an effort to escape, because they were rounding the curve all clumped together. If they had been suspicious, they would have been strung out, instead of offering themselves as a big single target. Among them was one wearing a wrinkled planter's hat.

"Pradier," Jessie said.

Ki nodded. "Looks like he sat on his hat."

"What's a few dents? It's right spiffy headgear," Thorpe said admiringly. "It'll make a spiffier bull's-eye any time now."

The trail filled with men. They came almost on top of the tree-lined section, and it began to resonate with their noise, but not their voices, for they were grim in their murderous intent. When they were filing in,

Jessie, Thorpe, and the others sighted their weapons—all except Ki, who avoided firearms unless they were the best choice. Earlier, at the mansion, he'd wanted range and noise, so he'd chosen a carbine. This place was so confining that he wanted close-quarters silence. So he readied his *shuriken*.

Pradier was little more than abreast of Thorpe now, and the slowpokes running drag were barely inside the gauntlet. Not yet... Not yet... Ki was still thinking "not yet" when one of the more impulsive Marines opened fire.

The man closest to Pradier abruptly jerked and keeled over. The next instant, fire poured forth from both sides. Pradier's men went every which way, sprawling, rolling, diving. Seven were killed outright. Three more toppled over and thrashed, knife-wounded, and two others were knocked down by their comrades seeking cover. They quickly recovered, however, and joined the rest in returning shots and rushing the shoulders of the trail.

Jessie feared what would happen if they let the men gain the trees; they couldn't afford either the time it would take to fight them in the undergrowth, or the risk of being split up and picked off one by one. To her relief, Lieutenant Lysander seemed also to realize that they'd have to make a stand here, out in the open, for she heard him order:

"Squad engage!"

The Marines sprang forward, counterattacking. Ki and Bonhomme grinned at each other from opposite sides, as they too leaped out into the trail. Captain Thorpe reared up, lumbering. Jessie came out swinging, and splintered the stock of her borrowed Henry

162

rifle across a man's skull. Lieutenant Lysander kicked her accidentally as he slashed his uniform saber at a redheaded man; when next Jessie glimpsed the man, his head was missing.

In such a melee, pistols were better than long-barreled weapons. Thorpe fired his Colt sidearm point-blank into one belly, then swiveled aside, firing again at a man coming up behind him. The man danced away toward the trees, his fingernails raking down the bark of the first one he reached as he fell dying. When three more ganged up on Thorpe, two were shot by Bonhomme and a Marine, the third removed by one of Ki's *shuriken*.

As he was retrieving his saber from a man's back, Lieutenant Lysander was smashed across the nose by a revolver butt. His nose was flattened, the cartilage crushed, blood spurting in torrents. But before the man who'd used his revolver like a polo club could finish the lieutenant off, one of his Marines put a neat black hole through the man's face with his service revolver. Ki crossed knives with a squat, dumpy man who was much more agile than he appeared. They closed in as if to hug each other, but in a deadly embrace. The man suddenly shuddered and staggered back, his free hand holding his chest, from which the handle of Ki's curved blade was protruding.

Ki withdrew his *tanto*, while glancing around for another man. There were only three or four left, and they were fighting savagely. But peripherally, almost accidentally, Ki caught sight of Pradier's planter's hat bobbing around the corner of the trail, as its owner scurried covertly back toward the landing.

"Pradier's making a break for it," Ki shouted to

163

Jessie. "He's running out on his own men. I'll be right back!"

Dodging by the last of the combatants, Ki sped along the path to the bend, which was quite sharp and led into a short straight stretch and another blind curve. Not entirely blind, however, for as he was entering the straight stretch, he perceived the heavy black silhouette of a man in a planter's hat, against the mouse-gray night air.

The silhouette moved, shifting, and Ki caught an instant's wink of something metallic. He swerved. There was a bark like a thunderclap, a lancing flame, but Pradier's ambushing shot flew so wild that Ki never heard where it went.

Headlong, Pradier surged around the curve and disappeared. Ki plunged after him, so preoccupied by pursuit that he ran oblivious to Jessie, then Thorpe chasing after him.

Heading into the curve, Ki spurted toward a narrow passage between high-canopied trees, and this length truly was dark. Pradier came into murky view momentarily as he crossed a bare patch, and Ki flicked a quick pass at him with a *shuriken*. The disk sawed into a huge bole less than a foot from Pradier's right sleeve, making him hasten to drop out of sight again. More worrisome to Ki was the distance; Pradier had been able to stretch his lead.

Ki reached the same bare patch, and in that instant he glimpsed—or intuited—the presence of Pradier a bit ahead. He didn't slow, he didn't stop; he backed rapidly away from that patch, while swiveling aside and abruptly dipping to one knee, grasping another *shuriken*. A rifle muzzle spat fire; Ki aimed for it and snapped. The rifle's sharp report and a blistering yowl blended with Jessie's startled cry as, hurrying to catch up with him, she smacked into his rucksack when he suddenly reversed.

She gasped. "Ki! Are you all right?"

He nodded, and spotted Thorpe hotfooting up. "You too? You should've stayed back there."

"Nobody left to fight." Thorpe grinned. "Our soldier boys'll be along, soon's they get Lysander's nose to working."

"I'm not waiting." Ki started out after Pradier again. When he saw that Jessie and Thorpe were keeping pace, he warned, "Careful! I wounded Pradier—I heard him yell—but I don't know how badly."

They passed the bare spot, where what light there was in the dim, cloudy sky shone down through a gap in the trees; and then they bounded deep into a darkness that was almost palpable.

When shortly they stumbled upon a blood-smeared rifle lying on the trail, Ki noted, "Well, Pradier won't be ambushing us with that anymore." But racing on, he feared that the trader was farther ahead than ever, and worse, was steadily increasing the distance. Pradier was no slouch to begin with, and was fresher, more rested than they, and wasn't encumbered by a heavy rucksack.

They pressed on faster, determined not to let Pradier elude them. Yet the winding trail stretched on endlessly through the dense growth, and the last section seemed to crawl by. Eventually they veered around the final bend and slid in mud, the path now flanking the water's edge. They heard an abrupt, high-pitched scream just as they were entering the wide, cleared field that served as the landing area.

The landing was deserted. Pradier had obviously
beat them here by a margin of some minutes. Diag-
onally to their left was a crude building obviously
used as a sort of haphazard depot and storehouse, but
it was so dark and silent that Ki doubted Pradier was
hiding in it. Beyond the building began the trail to
the mansion, which would be an even more foolish
place for a man trying to escape. And the scream had
come from their left, where the landing swept down
to the dock.

Without hesitating, they angled dockward across
the filed. The pier was barely more than a wooden
finger jutting out into the murky cove. Moored broadside to it was the pirated naval packet boat, a smaller
version of the cutter that had brought them to the
bayous. To the other side of the pier was attached a
long, very slender walkway of half-rotted planks and
posts; it strung out parallel to the bank for about three
hundred feet, for use as a mooring for flatboats and
such. At the moment the only craft tied to the pier
was at its far end: the little sidewheel paddleboat, so
venerable and dilapidated that it appeared hardly worth
stealing.

Steamy growth arched over the bank, preventing
a full view of the pier stretching away. It wasn't until
they were almost to the dock that they saw all of the
paddleboat . . .

And saw the cause of the scream: Von Eismann.

Standing on the deck of the tiny wheelhouse, the
Iceman was just finishing strangling Donetian Pradier.
His massive mechanical left hand was shaking Pradier
as a dog would a rat, his clawed fingers locked tight

166

around the Creole's throat. In his right fist was a thick Webley revolver. Glancing dockward at the onrushing trio, he swiftly took aim and fired.

A bullet snapped past Jessie, and another hummed between Ki and Thorpe as they all dove flat. Before they could recover, Von Eismann used his gunhand to rap a release mechanism of some sort, and then, swinging Pradier as his ratcheting fingers clicked open, he flung the broken-necked corpse overboard into the water.

Slipping on the gummy earth, the three darted, crouching, onto the dock. Von Eismann was barking orders to a couple of crewmen who were casting off lines down on the main deck; he fired a third time and missed, then lunged into the wheelhouse, slamming its door.

"I don't believe I saw what I just seed," Thorpe blurted, as Ki headed toward the pier with impetuous fury.

Jessie caught hold of Ki, forcing him to stop. "No! That pier is too thin, too long, too open! He'd pick you off in short order, if you tried to go out there after him."

"Well, I can't let him get away," Ki snapped. "If that's the only way to him, then that's the way I'll go."

"We can catch him with this," Thorpe suggested, jerking a thumb toward the packet, where smoke was issuing from its funnel. "Steam must be up, and it's faster'n his paddler."

"Hurry," Ki urged, and sprinted for its gangplank. "That's what Von Eismann's doing, you know, getting away."

Thorpe shook his head. "But why'd he kill Pradier?"

Running beside him, Jessie said, "Their plans got ruined, and somebody has to be blamed. Pradier's the scapegoat."

"Couldn't happen to a nicer gentleman."

On board, a hasty search located an engineer and two stokers. They wore Navy uniforms and ugly, scarred bruises, the effects of multiple beatings; and they were truly a skeleton crew, their bodies as gaunt and wasted as any in the prison compound. Nonetheless, the men grinned, game to try anything that would scuttle the enemy.

"Trouble is," the engineer explained, "the boilers ain't up to pressure. We had to keep 'em low-fired, only 'nough for controllin', y'see, not for propellin'."

"How long to get steam up?" Thorpe asked.

"A few minutes, if we hurry."

Ki, glancing across at the paddleboat, saw the waters on either side of it froth white as the paddles began to rotate. Drawing his knife, he hacked at his rucksack sling.

"What're you doing?" Jessie said.

"What I should have done to start with," he responded, the sack thudding to the deck. He launched into a furious dash toward the bow, where he leaped over the rail in a running dive, slicing cleanly into the water.

Jessie, sprinting after him, reached the bow rail just in time to see him surface. "Ki! You can't mean to swim there!" she called. But that was exactly what he was doing, stroking hard in the direction of the paddleboat, as it began to move sluggishly from the pier, belching black smoke.

She turned around to say something to Thorpe, but he too was going, accompanying the crew down to the boiler room. She looked back, but Ki had vanished in the darkness and rain.

Frustrated, she stalked after Thorpe, clambering below to find him shoveling coal in rhythmic coordination with the engineer and stokers. Flames leaped high as one of the stokers paused to widen the draft, and pressure needles started to tremble upward around their dials.

Thorpe stopped and wiped his brow. "There. I'll go cast off." Flashing a grin at Jessie, he scurried topside.

Jessie grabbed up his discarded shovel and began to throw coal, but the engineer waved her back, saying, "We got a handle on it now, ma'am. The cap'n will need extra eyes, so you go along to him. Go on!"

She clamped her lips, knowing it was impolite to swear in front of men, and returned to the main deck. Thorpe was tossing the stern line free, and as it splashed into the water below, he turned and gestured to her to follow him up to the pilothouse. By the time they were both inside it, she could feel the packet shudder and buck with renewed energy.

A moment later, the engine room telegraph clattered. Thorpe spun the wheel, and the bow slowly began to swing starboard, the packet's propeller spinning for a bite in the bayou water. The outline of the fleeing paddleboat was indistinct in the distance. There was no way to know if Ki had reached it, or if he hadn't, where he was instead.

"Keep a sharp eye peeled, Jessie. Warn me of

anything that looks like a log or whatever in our path."

"What could've possessed Von Eismann?" she wondered aloud, while peering out at the waters ahead. "Why didn't he arrange to take this packet, instead of that ancient teapot?"

"Well, this's faster and newer, but it's got a screw and draws more water. In a narrow channel he'd laugh at us, if he'd any idea what a paddler could do. I bet he does."

"*I* have no idea," she retorted. "Tell me!"

"It's got a paddle on either side, and an engine to power each paddle. With one wheel turning for'ard and the other reversed, a paddler will turn in its own length, while a packet like this'll wallow all 'round in a turn." Thorpe brought the bow up as the boat continued to gather speed. "Our best hope is to catch up and ram him before he can get on the open bayou. And be damn cautious doing it, too, else we'll go aground while he goes merrily splashing away."

She sighed. "Wonderful. And God knows where the cutter is lying offshore. At lease Von Eismann's staying close to shore."

"My guess is he'll keep close until he's around the curve of the island, then suck us in and head for open water, while we're trying not to cut the damn island in half. Why don't you fire off a few rounds, just to worry him some?"

"No rifle," she answered, for her borrowed Henry was still back at that last fight, its stock smashed, and Thorpe had not taken one along, either. Then she recalled that Ki had been carrying a carbine. Hurriedly she went down to the main deck, grabbed Ki's pack, and struggled up to the pilothouse. The pack was still

170

mostly intact, its rope and rawhide strips having been knotted and reknotted into a grotesque webbing that was virtually immune to unravelment.

When she managed to untangle the carbine, she yanked open a window and loosed several shots at the paddleboat's wheelhouse. They didn't appear to have any effect, so she closed the window. "Enough of that. Just a waste of good ammunition. Von Eismann's ignoring it, and if Ki's up there with him, it'd just be our fool luck to hit him instead."

"You can't really believe he swam aboard!"

"Captain Thorpe, I believe if anybody could, he did. I believe Ki felt so determined that he would've *walked* on the water to get at Von Eismann."

Chapter 17

Hindered by clothing, Ki plowed through the storm-choppy water and reached the paddleboat in a state of acute exhaustion. Frantically he searched for a grip, some handhold, anything to use so he could hoist himself aboard. But there was nothing, and the hull was slippery with algae.

His only hope, he realized, was to grab on to the cage that formed an arch over a paddlewheel. The churning paddles threw avalanches of water at him, boiling the surface around them like lava in a volcano. Three times he was repulsed. Three times he managed to rally his strength, and at last he caught a strut, held on, and, inch by inch, hoisted himself higher. Then, levering himself up with one knee, he climbed onto the timber that ran along the lower rib of the cage, stem to stern. At any moment, he knew, he might slip and be swept up by the heavy boards as they rotated, biting into the bayou water with increasing speed. If he'd hesitated one minute longer in diving from the packet, the paddleboat would have been too far ahead and going too fast for him to have boarded.

His arms felt as though they were ripping from their sockets, but slowly he shinnied up to the rail and rolled onto the main deck, where he crouched behind a coil of hawser.

Peering aft, he could see that the packet was finally under way, but was not yet up to the sidewheeler's pace. Then, turning his attention to the boat he was on, he realized it was markedly different from Thorpe's sternwheeler. The engines were amidships of the main deck, not aft and below; they were set between the paddles, with their boilers and fireboxes fitted behind. Two men were heaving coal and a third was manipulating a bank of levers; there appeared to be a bank of these for each wheel, with a complicated linking mechanism so they could operate together or separately. The din of the hissing boilers and clanking machinery and rotating wheels was deafening, and that, he figured, was in his favor.

Heartily wishing he knew more about boats, Ki eased from behind the coiled hawser rope, and began to stealthily approach the crewmen. By the dim light of oil lanterns and the glare from the fireboxes, they were black with coal and glistening with sweat. They were also Von Eismann's stooges, Ki judged; Von Eismann didn't trust anyone much, but he certainly wouldn't trust prisoners to run things down here while he was stuck in the wheelhouse above. Besides which, the one working the machinery was armed.

So the first order of battle was to eliminate the crew.

Hunching low, Ki glided noiselessly toward the chinless man at the machinery. Before he could reach him, the man left his controls and sauntered toward the stokers, saying, "Roger, I think p'raps you got a buildup on the grates."

The taller of the stokers nodded, and stuck his shovel into the firebox to root around in the ashes. The three men were more or less grouped together now, much to Ki's liking. He closed to within a few feet on his silent, moccasinlike slippers, and was calculating his triple play when the tall stoker removed a shovel-load of glowing embers and turned to go toss them overboard. And saw Ki bearing down on them.

"Holy shit!" he blurted. And the chinless man pivoted, drawing his revolver. "A stowaway! I'll plug the critter!"

While he was squeezing the trigger, Ki was launching himself across the intervening deck in a *tobi-geri* flying kick. Ki's extended right foot smashed into the man's solar plexus, buckling him and flinging him backwards to the rail, where he cracked his spine and toppled over into the water.

Ki, meanwhile, had landed springing on his left foot, swiveled, and kicked out again with his right. The toe of his slipper caught the underlip of the tall stoker's shovel, flipping it up and showering red-hot clinkers into the stoker's face and torso. Flailing his arms, the stoker started to scream. He stopped his scream when Ki followed through with a *mae-geri-keage*—a forward snap-kick—which caved in the man's ribs.

174

By then the other stoker was rushing in, swatting at Ki with a skull-crushing iron poker. Ducking the wild swings, Ki grabbed the stoker's outflung arm, then angled to drop to one knee, propelling the stoker into a kneeling shoulder-toss, which catapulted him arcing through the air. The stoker came down flat and sprawled supine, dazed and breathless.

Punting the poker aside, Ki grabbed the stoker by the bib of his overalls, hauled him upright, and slammed him against the nearest bulkhead. "Show me how the controls work!"

Although fearful, the man stubbornly shook his head no.

Ki chopped the edge of one hand down on the stoker's nose. He purposely held back a little so he wouldn't break it, but struck forcefully enough to hurt like hell, and tears of pain welled in the man's eyes. "Show me how this tub works!"

The stoker capitulated to Ki's demands. In a quavering voice he pointed out two of the levers, gesturing their purpose. Ki nodded. Seconds later he understood the reverse throttles. He thought a moment, then demanded, "What happens if they go opposite ways?"

"The boat just spins where it is. Goes nowhere."

"Make it do that."

"Which way?"

"I don't care! Any damn way!"

"Well...I ain't the engineer, y'know," the stoker hedged, but he fumbled with the levers in a frenzy to please Ki. He produced a bit more results than had been asked for.

Overstressed gears and shafts shuddered, screamed,

and chattered protests. The portside wheel seemed to lock in place, snapping some of its paddles, and then began a violent thrashing in the opposite direction. The entire vessel shook itself, threatening to pop ribs and timbers, and began a dizzy rotation around the axis of its paddlewheels.

"You did fine," Ki said, and by way of congratulation he gripped the stoker by the seat of the pants and the scruff of the neck, ran him to the rail, and tossed him overboard.

The tall stoker was dead, Ki saw as he glanced around. The engineer had gone swimming with pistol still in hand, and the poker was not the best of all possible weapons. So Ki started after the Iceman with just what he'd arrived with.

In addition to being of a different design, the sidewheeler was also much smaller than the *Dauphine*. It was roughly seventy feet overall, with a beam of about twenty-five feet, Ki estimated; and it had no Texas deck atop the salon and main decks, but only a wheelhouse. Logically, Von Eismann would be topside, either steering himself or giving orders to a helmsman in the wheelhouse—but Ki suspected there might be an encounter before he climbed that far, for the Iceman would surely be curious about the boat's misbehavior.

His guess was almost immediately confirmed. He had reached the salon deck promenade, and had just located the ladder to the wheelhouse, when the hard, heavy bulk of Von Eismann plunged down at him from out of the dark night.

Evidently Von Eismann realized he had company only a fraction of a second before they collided. But he was swift, as swift and alert as anyone Ki had faced

176

since the death of his samurai master, Hirata. When Ki, with his curved-blade knife already in hand, slashed in to disembowel him, Von Eismann swerved and slapped Ki's knife hand aside.

Just as quickly, Ki countered with a left-handed chop to Von Eismann's exposed neck. Von Eismann caught the chop with an upsweep of his right arm, his human arm, while driving a *yonhon-nukite* blow to Ki's belly with his stiffened metal fingers. Ki leaped backwards and to one side, the lethal hand searing past his midriff, and simultaneously launched a sideways elbow smash in an effort to burst the Iceman's heart. He winced, pain blazing from his elbow joint to his shoulder; Von Eismann had on his bulletproof cast-iron breastplate again.

The sheer hammering force of his elbow smash, however, rocked Von Eismann back a pace. It gave Ki some room, a respite, and he used it to snap-kick with savage precision. Von Eismann shifted to protect his groin; anticipating this defense, Ki angled his kick to strike the kneecap. Von Eismann lurched as his leg collapsed under him, and before he could recover, Ki moved in to stab him in the throat.

Swearing gutturally in German, Von Eismann caught the knifeblade at the instant it was pricking the skin of his larynx. One second, less than a second more! Ki raged inwardly, so furious he could hardly see straight, and adamantly kept trying to plunge it in, forcing it against Von Eismann's throat.

But Von Eismann had captured the blade in his steel fingers, and was able to struggle enough to resist the harsh pressure Ki was exerting. His right-hand fingers clawed at Ki's face, the nails scraping his

177

cheeks, trying for his eyes. All the while they were pushing and tugging each other, twisting within each other's grasp in a strange *danse macabre* that sent them careening along the deck from rail to bulkhead and back. Ki pressed harder, hearing the raspy breath, seeing the blue-mottled features writhing, mouth snarling.

Then they hit the salon deck rail for the last time. Still wrapped in their lethal embrace, they bowled over the side and plummeted to the main deck below, smacking against its wooden planks.

"What in the name o' the Holy Virgin is happenin' over there?" Thorpe yelled, staring out the window.

The packet had approached within a couple of hundred yards of the paddleboat, which for some unfathomable reason was spinning around, going nowhere fast. Two men could be glimpsed fighting on its upper deck whenever, like a carousel, it twirled into view. The big white-haired Prussian and Ki were kicking and gouging and slashing at each other, while reeling and stumbling precariously around.

"Ki needs help," Jessie declared. "That's what's happening over there. Get there, get us aboard!"

"I can't! Shoot the big fellow!"

"Are you crazy? They're closer together than Siamese twins, Greg, and no telling which I'd hit. Let me think . . ."

She glanced about while she frantically ran through a mental list of what she knew was available. The packet was supposedly loaded with ordnance, but she didn't have the time, much less the training, to figure out what might work. Pistols and rifles were useless, as were knives—even if either of them could toss a knife that far. Nothing much good in Ki's pack either, just a few sacks of gunpowder. Dynamite sticks and caps and fuse. Fishing line. A bow and some arrows.

Bow and arrow?

An idea was born full-grown. Grinning wickedly, Jessie hunched by the pack, pawing through it for the dynamite and fishing line. "Move in as close as you can, Greg," she ordered, as she wrapped the dynamite sticks to the arrows with fishing line. Explosives weren't her trade, but she knew enough to know how to wedge in the caps, and resorted to plain guessing to estimate the length of fuse to use.

"Now a match," she said, picking up the bow and the first arrow. Thorpe looked at her as if he thought she'd lost her senses, but handed her his waterproof tin of block matches and hastily opened a window when he saw her light the dynamite fuse.

"Greg, I don't see them now. Where are they?"

"They fell off. They're on the main deck."

"Damn!" she swore. Notching the arrow to the bowstring, she drew steadily until the bow was deeply curved, then let fly.

The arrow went sailing up and away, arcing nicely toward the paddleboat. They both watched anxiously as it curved downward and landed on the promenade deck, bouncing once and then just lying there, sparking.

"The fuse is too long," she said, and clipped the next one accordingly before lighting it and sending it streaking after the first. "This one ought to be better."

"Have you any notion what you're doing?"

"I placed second in after-dinner archery at Saratoga

Springs last season," she retorted. "Ki needs some way of getting clear of Von Eismann long enough for me to shoot. The dynamite ought to rattle Von Eismann at least that much, don't you think? Besides, have you got a better idea?"

Shaking his head lamely, Thorpe watched with Jessie as her second arrow followed a similar trajectory. But the paddleboat had swung broadside to them, and instead of hitting high, where its explosion couldn't injure Ki while it was startling Von Eismann, the arrow nosed down at the edge of the cargo area. There was an almost instantaneous eruption that lit the sky. Bits of the boat flew in all directions, yet it kept turning as if nothing serious had been damaged.

And by the explosion's sudden flare, Jessie glimpsed Ki and the Iceman continuing their fight on the main deck. So she lit and strung a third arrow, adjusting her aim.

Von Eismann couldn't pivot his mechanical hand, because something inside its wrist mechanism had snapped when he'd used it to break his fall. Yet he could still swing his arm, and had managed to knock Ki's knife from his grasp, the blade dropping underfoot, swallowed by the dark, dense action of their struggle. His hard, cropped skull crunched against Ki's jaw and raked his nose, sending blood flying. Ki scraped his fingers in the Iceman's white hair, and then brought the edge of his other hand across to pay him back in kind. There was the satisfying crunch of a nose breaking, and only the quick averting of his head saved Von Eismann from having his brain pierced with slivers of bridge bone and cartilage.

180

He responded by thrusting his meaty right hand against Ki's loins and wrenching at his genitals in a vicious, viselike grip. Ki almost blacked out, nearly puking on Von Eismann as they kept on rolling in a tight ball together around the main deck. Only dimly did he perceive the shattering roar of Jessie's second dynamite-laden arrow, and he certainly wasn't aware of what had caused the inexplicable demise of the cargo area. His world was momentarily confined to the squeezing clutch between his legs, and the searing agony spiraling up from his belly.

"Vas ist los?" Von Eismann barked, glancing up, inadvertently relaxing his hold on Ki as he realized what was going on.

In desperation, Ki yanked his arm back and poked stiffened fingers directly into Von Eismann's eyes. He could feel the sockets warm and moist, and then Von Eismann was falling away. Panting, grimacing from pain, Ki scrambled frantically up, his every instinct centered on killing the now sobbing Iceman.

Then he glimpsed what Von Eismann had been bellowing about. Across in the dimly lit pilothouse of the nearby packet, Jessie had just released another rocketing arrow. He could see its curve, could estimate its point of impact, and he realized if he stayed long enough to kill Von Eismann, he'd most likely wind up dead as well.

He tore pell-mell toward the rail and leaped over the side, reluctantly leaving Von Eismann writhing blinded on the deck. And Jessie's third arrow winged through the open door of one of.the boilers' fireboxes.

Ki was still diving toward the water when suddenly there was no more paddleboat. It did not break, it did

181

not sink, it simply disintegrated. Simultaneously there was a screeching, ripping burst and a phosphorescent white wash of light as the firebox split like a rotten tomato, rupturing the other, their flaming innards spewing in cartwheeling shrapnel. Both boilers shattered in a cushion of fire, then geysered straight up with a raining cascade, igniting the salon deck and wheelhouse. Cabins mushroomed one by one, flinging shards of glass and metal in all directions, puncturing the hold and sending the main deck into a lake of explosive flame.

The first dynamite stick then detonated, and with it a somewhat human shape was lifted, flapping and somersaulting, to disappear into the night sky and bayou mists. Fresh winds blew a curtain of thick black smoke across the scene, bringing with it more pelting rain.

Ki found himself floating on the dank water's surface, stunned. Around him, chunks of the paddleboat were tumbling, shattered and burnt. The boat itself was merely a hull burning furiously, enveloped in smoke. And his ears were still ringing, deafened from the concussion.

It was ten minutes before Ki, treading water, was spotted and hauled aboard the packet. Thorpe made a few passes around the burning wreck of the sidewheeler, then headed back to the landing.

"Von Eismann may be out there alive," Ki warned.

"We saw him blown sky-high," Jessie assured him. "Stood right here in the pilothouse, and saw his li'l ol' body sail away, like a limp rag doll."

"And dead or alive, there's not a chance in hell of finding him in this stuff," Thorpe said. "We'll look

182

again come daylight, when we can get some help."

Somehow, Ki suspected it wouldn't do much good.

At sunrise, the packet and the cutter began a fruitless search of the bayou for Von Eismann's body. The remains of the dead raiders were noted, and those few who'd managed to survive the night were clapped into irons for eventual transport to prison.

Thorpe took Jessie aside and said, "There'll be a lot of paperwork and inquiry on this. Your testimony will be important. And *Dauphine*'s in for overhaul at Baton Rouge. You might want to spend some time here."

"Here?" She smiled lightly. "I'd prefer to survive a stay in New Orleans."

Ki, too, felt the desire to be away from this remote and mysterious world of its own. Annette had returned with her father to his small settlement, but her absence was not the cause of his chaffing. Bonhomme Richard had also departed for his home, but Ki didn't feel frustrated by the loss of a drinking and bullshit partner.

Instead, he stood alone at the edge of the dock, and gazed out over the bayou cove in the direction of the paddleboat's still smoldering debris. Von Eismann's boat, the boat that had become his funeral pyre. And Ki knew that the sooner he left Orange Island, the sooner he'd stop nursing the idiotic urge to keep searching, keep hunting, until he had the corpse and was absolutely certain it was true. But of course it was true; everyone said so.

The Iceman was gone for good—again.

Dead—again.

Sure.

183